Bob Moats

I0567327

Lonely Hearts Murders

By Bob Moats

Rev. 052815-1505

Lonely Hearts Murders

For information and address:
Magic 1 Productions
P.O. Box 524, Fraser MI 48026-0524
Website: http://murdernovels.com

Cover design by Bob Moats

~~*~~

Bob Moats

Lonely Hearts Murders

Kennel Murders
Trick or Treat Murders
Santa Murders
Wiseguy Murders
Toxic Murders
Private Eye Murders

For a preview or to purchase a book, go to
http://murdernovels.com

What a few people are saying about Murder Novels by Bob Moats

Mr. Moats, I just got your novel "Classmate Murders" and have to let you know, I read it in one evening. That is the first book I have ever done that with. That was the most enjoyable book I have ever read. I just started reading e-books, and reading again, after getting my wife a Kindle. This book was my 12th, and the best. I just got Las Vegas Showgirls to (read) tomorrow evening. I look forward to reading many of your books in this series. I have been searching for an author and books that were fun, entertaining reads. Your books are just the ticket.

Regards, A new fan, Bill from South Carolina

****

Another very nice comment submitted through my website from Micki P.:

"I recently was given a kindle for my 60th birthday. The first book I downloaded was the Classmate Murders and have now read every one of them. Today I started on the Fatal Rejection series. Thank you for the wonderful ride with Jim and Penny and all the rest of the troop. I have laughed and giggled thru the stories, my poor family gave me the strangest looks! Now I really want a little Yorkie!! Fatal Rejection so far is another great read! I will be looking out for more of Jim Richards and since you are my #1 Author, anything of yours I can find."

Extra special thanks to:

To Susan Haughton, for editing my chapters and putting up with my taking too long to get them done.

To the beta readers for proofing the final copy and hopefully catching all those annoying little errors that slip through. To all the great people who read my books and sent comments to me about them.

A special thanks to my Facebook friends who entered one of my silly little contests to have their names used in this book. Here's to George Conner, Lisa Keller, Sue Hanson, Kathy Teems Jones, Jack Plunkitt, Sherry Faller Byrne, and Paul and Lynette Lawrance.

Thank you to all the people who purchased this book. I hope you enjoy it as much as I enjoyed writing it for my faithful readers.

The Jim Richards Family of Readers is listed in the back of the book.

~~*~~

Lonely Hearts Murders

by Bob Moats

Chapter 1

I was surprised to see my daughter, Carol, standing at my office door. I was also surprised that Lacey hadn't made a big deal out of her being in the building. My office manager would never pass up a detail like Carol being here, without warning me.

"What are you doing here? You're always so busy at Angelo's cooking up a storm." I asked.

"I know, but I have a problem and I hoped you could help," she said, moving into my room. She looked worried and then sat in my client chair.

Lonely Hearts Murders

"Okay, I'm here for you, tell me what's up?" I turned my attentions to her and waited. She now looked distressed. I continued to wait, giving her the time to let it out.

She finally said, "I have a friend who may be in trouble."

"What kind of trouble?" I asked when she stopped talking.

"That's just it, I don't know. She's missing." She went silent again, wringing her hands and looking at the floor.

"Carol, have you talked to the police?"

"I don't have anything to give them. No evidence that she's actually missing, or how long she's been gone."

"Okay, start at the beginning. Who is your friend and why do you believe she's missing?"

"Her name is Lisa Keller, I've known her for about a month. She was a new employee at Angelo's, working as a waitress. We got along well and she was a very nice person. She didn't come into work two days ago and since then has been missing. She has no family here in Las Vegas, so there was no one to report her missing."

"I presume she had no friends?"

"Just me and two of the other girls at the restaurant. I talked to them and they don't know where she is. I know she's new in town, but to just disappear like that, so soon after starting a job, it's not right."

"Tell me about her. Whatever you know, or she told you."

"Well, she came from a town in Indiana and moved here about three months ago. She saw the ad that Angelo put in the Review-Journal for a waitress position. She told Angelo that she had experience and he hired her. She was a happy person most of the time, but she told me she was lonely without having someone, a man, to share with. She said she had a boyfriend back home but they broke up. So she moved here for the excitement and glamor."

"Boy, was she wrong," I said. My tiny toy Yorkie, Willy, came rushing in the room and over to Carol. She reached down and picked him up.

"Hey, baby, how are you doing?" she asked as Willy was trying to lick her hands. Carol laughed and looked back to me. "Do you think you could see if she's all right?"

"Well, I don't have much to do lately, so I could give it a quick look. Do you know her address?" I asked.

She dug into her purse and pulled out a card. She handed it to me. "She gave me this after we started to get to know each other a little better. I hope you can find out what happened to her."

"I'll do my best, but she may have decided that she didn't like Vegas and went back home. Or found a different job."

"I don't think she would do either of those things without talking to me. We had a nice bond together."

"We all have things that we don't share with others, so don't feel bad if she didn't confide everything to you," I said.

"I know, I guess it was nice to have a friend to talk to. I've been so busy at the restaurant, I haven't had much time to get to know anyone. Besides, in Vegas there aren't many places to find a friend. Although Lisa did mention a place that helped lonely people. It's a match type company for people looking for dates."

"Those places are just as bad as meeting people in a bar. They never look into a person very carefully, just a few questions and a photograph, then they set a person up with whomever has the money to look through the photos of other lonely people."

"You sound like you've been there," Carol said with a grin.

"Okay, in my youth, I tried a couple of the dating places. I also paid a small fortune for nothing. I did better in a bar."

"Did what better in a bar?" came a voice from my door. It was Penny. She always popped up when I said something incriminating. Just so she could interrogate me. She breezed into the room and over to Carol. "Carol, it's so good to see you outside of the restaurant. Have a day off finally?"

"I'm starting to cut back on my hours. Angelo is not happy, but he understands I can't die in the kitchen."

"Are you just visiting or have a crime for Jim to solve?" Penny asked, sitting next to Carol. She reached over to take Willy, who was squirming.

"I have a small problem, maybe. I thought maybe Dad could help."

"What is it?" Penny asked.

"A missing friend," I answered her. "I'm going to check out the friend and see if she's all right."

"Good, I have nothing better to do today, I'll go with you," Penny said with a smile.

I cringed at the thought, but it couldn't hurt to take her. She could come up with good ideas that often helped to solve cases. Not that I hoped this would become a case. I hoped the missing woman was just doing something better than being a waitress. "Fine, you can come with me."

"Good that you made up your mind. When do we go?"

"Be patient. Carol, what are you going to do today?"

"I have to go into work, since Lisa left we're a little short of help. Angelo told me after Lisa comes back, if she does, he'd give me a week off for vacation. I haven't taken a break since I've been there. I do love to cook, and the people there are so nice, I hate to leave."

"If you enjoy your job, it's hard to get away," I said. "I know, I like my job so well, I rarely take vacations. The one that Penny and I took to travel around the country doing my book signing was nice, but it was work related. I'd just like to go relax and not think of crime and writing books."

Penny added, "I enjoy doing my TV show, and would hate to go away. They'd probably find out I could be replaced easily enough. So I keep at it."

"I should be going, I'll call you later and see if you found out anything." She stood and said her goodbyes.

We watched her leave and Penny turned to me. "Where's Lacey? I came through the lobby and she wasn't there."

"I don't know. I haven't been out of my office this morning. She wasn't out there?"

"No, I stood in the lobby and waited, but she's missing."

"Great, more missing persons. Is this an epidemic?" I said and stood. I went out followed by Penny and Willy, heading for the front lobby

The desk where Lacey held court was empty, which I thought was odd. She hardly ever left the desk for very long. I called her name loudly and listened. Then I heard a small voice coming from the doorway to the side offices, where Lynn, Deacon and Buck were located. Along with the break room and lounge.

"I'm busy," was the reply from behind the door. That sounded like Lacey's demanding voice.

"Are you all right?" I yelled back. The door opened and she came out followed by a bouquet of helium balloons, one of which said 'Happy Birthday.' She tied them to her chair.

"Now, do you need me?" she asked.

"Uh, whose birthday is it?" I asked.

"Jessie, I found out when she was born and it's today."

**

Chapter 2

"We have to get a present for her," Penny said to me, then turned to Lacey. "Are you having a party for her here or at your home?"

"Lynn and I are getting the lounge all decorated up and Mac is going to bring her here this afternoon. Everyone is invited."

"You should have given every one more time so they can get presents," Penny said.

"I told everyone yesterday. Well, you and Jim were gone all day, so you didn't hear. It was a last minute thing."

"Well, don't start without us," Penny said and turned to me. "Let's go shopping."

Now I was visualizing her in the mall taking forever to find something. "Why don't we just go to K-Mart?" I asked hopefully.

She thought on that. "Right, we don't have a lot of time. Let's move it." She pushed me to the back door where our cars were.

On the way to the store Penny said, "We can check on Carol's friend after the party."

I couldn't disagree with her although I wanted to start right away. I always seem to get caught up in the plans of others. I think that's why I liked to hide away in the office.

Lonely Hearts Murders

We attacked the store and got her some nice tops, which Penny picked out. We found some gift boxes and went back to the office. Penny went with Lynn to wrap the gifts as I stood with the men in the lounge looking at all the streamers and decorations.

Buck grinned and said, "Think you guys could do this for my birthday?"

Earl, Trapper, Deacon, and I all said we doubted it. Buck laughed, "Just don't forget my birthday at least."

An hour later, Mac came in with Jessie and we surprised her. She burst into tears and then we celebrated. She opened all the gifts everyone brought and told us she loved us all. Lacey and Mac got her a game console and a nice watch. I knew that she had her own cell phone, Mac didn't want her to be without one in case of emergency. Lynn and Deacon got her an mp3 player so she could store all her music on it to listen to. Earl, Trapper and Buck went together and bought a dozen games for her console. So, she was in heaven.

A short while later, Lynn and Lacey were cleaning up the room as Jessie sat playing with her gifts. Penny said to me that we should go look for the missing girl. I went to Jessie and wished her a happy birthday, then quietly slipped her a hundred dollar bill and told her not to tell her mother. Lacey probably would take it and put it in savings. "Spend it on yourself," I said and kissed her in the top of her head. She grinned and thanked me.

I told Lacey that we had to go find a missing girl and took Penny out of the room. We went out to the car and drove away.

I pulled out the card with Lisa Keller's address on it and handed it to Penny. "See if you can find out where this is on your phone's Google. I know the street crossroads, at least."

Penny took out her smartphone, brought up Google maps and located the house. She told me where to go so I headed there. It was an apartment building and it was run down, looking like it was on the verge of being condemned. Or so it seemed.

I parked and we went to the front door of the apartment number on the card. I knocked since there was no doorbell, and waited. I knocked again and still no answer. I stood there looking around when I saw an unmarked police cruiser pull into the lot. The car parked next to mine and Detective Greg Warren got out.

He came up to us and smiled. "Jim, Penny, what are you doing here?" he asked.

"My daughter, Carol, was concerned that her friend, Lisa Keller, has been missing. She asked me to find her."

Greg looked serious and said, "I can tell you where she is. She's in the morgue. Sorry."

I was shocked and asked, "How did she die?"

"It's an ongoing investigation, but I'm sure you know that. Oh, hell, Jim, she died of a gunshot to the head. Her body was found behind the Flamingo hotel."

I looked at Penny and her expression was sadness. "I'd hate to tell Carol," Penny said.

"I'll do it," I replied. "What are you doing here?" I asked Greg.

"My job. Investigating the murder. I came here to examine the home environment. I have her keys," he said.

"Where's CSI?"

"On their way. I called after I left the morgue." Greg went to the door and opened it with the key. He swung the door inward and stood at the doorstep.

"Are you going in?" I asked him.

"I don't want to contaminate the scene before they examine it," he said with a grin. "I suppose you'll want to check it out?"

"It would be nice," I replied. "But we can wait."

The forensic van drove in and three men and one woman got out. Greg gave them the details about the case as I stood listening. Penny said she was going to sit in the car, and went out there.

The CSI team went to work in the apartment as I watched from the door. Greg was inside taking evidence bags and labeling them. He was close to me now and I asked, "So, anything?"

"Nothing for you, Jim. You know better," Greg said.

"If Deacon or Lynn were still on the force handling this case, they would have told me," I said with a smirk.

"Well, I'm not Deacon or Lynn. I'm trying for the Lieutenant slot and I don't want to queer my chances. So stop asking," he said and then spoke quietly, "I'll give you what I have, later, please."

"I got it," I said and told him I would talk later. I went to the car and got in.

"So?" Penny asked.

"Greg's being careful with facts. His promotion is on the line and he doesn't want to mess it up."

"Well, he deserves the promotion for all he's been through. Especially during the toxic poisoning case where they had that creep lieutenant brought in. Greg should have gotten the job."

"I agree with that. But that was bureaucratic injustice. Greg will finally get the slot. But it will take him going by the book now. Then he can screw around, after."

"Like Lynn and Deacon did," Penny said.

"Right," I said, "Let's go talk to Carol and Angelo."

Lonely Hearts Murders

I drove over to Mama Mia restaurant and parked. Angelo was at the door, greeting guests.

"Jim, Penny! Good to see youse," he said, in his best mob vernacular.

"Angelo, we need to talk to you and Carol, in private, if possible."

"Why sure, Mr. R., give me a minute to get Carol and we can go into my office," he said and went off.

We stood looking at all the people eating food and enjoying themselves. "I'm glad I helped Angelo get this restaurant going. It's been a real success," I said to Penny.

"Yes, business has really picked up with all the publicity and ads you've been doing," she said.

"Yep, have to let the public know it's here and the food is great," I replied. "I've even put Angelo's face on taxi-top ads all over Vegas. His face is seen now more than the Blue Man Group," I said with a grin.

Angelo came out of the kitchen followed by Carol. He waved to us and motioned toward his office. We went into the room, sitting on his chairs. Carol was looking concerned. She probably figured that since we needed Angelo along, it wasn't good news.

I leaned towards Carol and said, "I'm sorry, Carol, but it's not good. We went to Lisa's apartment and found the police there. Lisa was murdered."

**

Chapter 3

"Oh, no!" she exhaled. She started to tear up and Penny gave her a tissue from a box on Angelo's desk.

"I'm sorry to be so blunt, but I can't think of any other way to say it," I said.

"When, how?" Carol asked.

"I don't know the details yet, they're still investigating. I will find out, though, and I'll make it a goal to find out who did this."

"Thank you, Dad," she said, wiping her eyes.

I looked at Angelo and he said, "Guess I need a new waitress. This is not good. She was a sweet girl. If you need my connections in the family, let me know."

I knew exactly what Angelo meant. He still had a lot of connections to his family back in New York, but through word of mouth he had built up a modest family of former mob figures here in Vegas. There were a lot of wiseguys still hanging out in Sin City, even though the mobs lost their hold on the casinos long ago. I didn't want to bring any of them in, but they were helpful in the past. "Thanks, my friend, I'll let you know."

I didn't have much more to say. Angelo told Carol to take the rest of the day off. He knew that Lisa and Carol had become friends.

"No, I need to work to take my mind off this. But thanks." She stood and left the room.

"You don't know anything?" Angelo asked.

"No, Greg Warren is on the case and he can't tell me anything yet."

"Well, remember what I said. My network of family can find out a lot of things involving crime."

"I know you can, and I'll remember that, when I need help. Thanks again." Penny and I stood and left the room.

Outside I turned to Penny, "I need to pick Warren's brain and get what they have. I may even talk to Captain Weber if need be. I need to find this killer, for Carol."

"I know you will, Jim. I'll even leave you alone to work this case." She kissed me and we went to the car. I drove out and back to the office.

As I was walking down the hallway, I stopped at the office doors of Trapper and Earl asking them to join me in my office. I went in and called Deacon, Lynn and Buck, asking them to join me.

Everyone was in the room as Deacon said, "Are you closing the firm?"

I laughed and said, "No, we're good. I need to ask any of you who aren't working a case right now to help me with one." I explained what I had and Trapper, along with Deacon, said they'd help. The others were on cases, so I thanked them and said to go to work. They left as Deacon and Trapper sat waiting.

"Greg Warren has the info from the woman's apartment and the crime scene but he isn't sharing. He's too worried about his promotion to let me get involved. I don't blame him, it's important to him. If we can find this killer, let's give him the credit."

Both Trapper and Deacon agreed. Deacon spoke first, "Maybe I can talk to Greg and see what he has. He may loosen up with me."

"Give it a try. I don't know exactly where the body was found, except it was behind the Flamingo Hotel. Trapper and I can go look that over, while you visit Greg. I want this killer, so let's do our best."

They agreed and we left my office. Deacon went to his office as Trapper and I went to my car.

"We need to check out the crime scene before LVPD messes it up," Trapper said. He was once a cop in Vegas so he still knew a number of officers and higher-ups, more than I did. He and Captain Weber had a love-hate relationship that had provided me with lots of laughs over the past few years we had been here in Vegas. Especially when Penny and I came out here from Michigan to get married. Trapper and Barry Becker had a ball pulling pranks on Weber.

"I hope Greg will loosen up with Deacon. I'd like to get some facts," I said.

"Greg has been the whipping boy for far too long. Williams is an idiot and probably would never be promoted past junior grade detective. I think Greg has a good chance as long as they don't bring in someone from another division."

"I know Weber wanted Greg in the lead, back when Deacon left the force. But command brought in Boering and forced them to put him in the position. I'm sure command regretted that decision after what Boering did."

"I see police tape," Trapper said as we pulled in behind the Flamingo Hotel. I pulled into the parking area for RV and camper guests to put their larger vehicles. I shut off the car and we got out, walked over to where the tape was trying to keep people away. There were tourists gawking just outside the perimeter taking pictures. Everyone has a cellphone now and photos and video were a way of life for most people. They usually ended up on Facebook to bore others to death.

We walked through the area and up to the tape. I looked around and couldn't see any police milling about. I figured they cleared the crime scene and left. There probably wouldn't be anything for us to see, CSI most likely took everything incriminating. I ducked under the tape and moved to the bushes where there were markers probably signifying where the body was located.

Lonely Hearts Murders

"No excessive amounts of blood, so this must have been a dump site," Trapper said.

"Why here? This is a public throughway, the killer had to have figured someone would find the body. He had to move fast to drop the body and get away before being seen. The body was left well off the drive." I looked up, and spotted two security cameras on poles overlooking the area we were in.

I pointed to the cameras and said, "I'm sure CSI has already gotten the video from those. It would be a waste of time to talk to hotel security to get the video now. I hope Deacon can get something for us."

While we stood in the crime scene, two hotel security officers came over to us. "Gentlemen, this is a closed crime scene, if you could leave the area."

"Derrick?" Trapper said.

"Will, is that you? Damn, you got old," the man said.

"Not half as old as you look. You working for the hotel now?"

"I'm supervisor for security. It's an easy gig. What are you doing?"

"I'm a private investigator with my friend here, Jim Richards," Trapper replied.

The man looked at me and smiled, "Sure, Jim Richards, you're a well-known celebrity around here. Good to meet you." He held out his hand to shake, I took it.

"Are you investigating this murder?" Derrick asked.

"My daughter was a friend of the victim. I'm making it a goal to find the killer. Anything you can tell us that the police got from the area?"

"After we called to report the body, LVPD rolled in and took over. It's our property, so I insisted that we be on-site. They weren't happy, but they cooperated. I didn't get much other than the body was dumped here. Our cameras did get a look at the vehicle, but I heard them say it was stolen. They couldn't see the face of the killer either. He kept his face well hidden."

"A bust all around," I said.

**

Chapter 4

"I'm afraid so," Derrick said. "Wish I could help you, Jim. If I hear anything, I can call you."

I gave him my card and Trapper gave the man his. We said our goodbyes and left the area. In the car we sat thinking. Then I asked Trapper, "How do you know Derrick?"

"We were both on the force together back when I was a bicycle cop here in Vegas. We patrolled the Strip and got in trouble frequently," he replied with a grin.

"Involving hookers, I presume," I said.

"No comment, but yes. Derrick was a lot like me, crazy in the head. We pulled a lot of stunts with the tourists. I was surprised we weren't caught," he said with a smile. "Now, what are we going to do?"

"I have no idea, since we have no evidence and there seems to be nothing to go on so far. Let's go see what Deacon found out."

"From what you said, the victim was a friend of the other waitresses at Angelo's. Maybe she shared things with them that she didn't with your daughter." Trapper said.

I thought on that. It was a valid point. "Okay, we can go talk to the girls and see what their opinions are." I turned the car to go to Angelo's and after a short drive, pulled into the parking lot.

We entered the restaurant but Angelo was not at the door. A girl, Sherry Byrne, who was the actual greeter, smiled and came to us. "Hello, Mr. Richards and Mr. Trapper. Dinner for two?"

I grinned at her proper greeting and said, "No, thank you. Is Angelo in?"

She smiled and said, "He left for the day. He said he needed the time to visit with his lady friend."

"I thought he broke up with her, or she broke up with him, whatever."

"This is a new girlfriend, her name is Raphaela. He met her through a friend. He's trying to give her enough attention so as not to screw up like he did with the last girlfriend. But I didn't say that, so just ignore me."

"No problem, Sherry. We just need to talk to a few people who were friends or acquaintances of Lisa Keller."

"Oh, poor Lisa. I feel so bad," she said.

"Did you know her very well?" I asked.

"I got to know her, yes. We talked a lot when it was slow."

"Could you sit with us and answer a few questions?"

"I suppose I could." She turned and pulled over the stand with a sign saying 'Please seat yourself.'

"Shall we go into the banquet room? It's quiet in there," I said.

She agreed and took us to the room. She closed the door after we entered and we went to a table and sat. I didn't want to rush her, so she could relax before I asked my questions.

Lonely Hearts Murders

"I'm a little emotional about Lisa's death. This is new to me as I've never had a person close to me that was murdered. Go ahead and ask your questions, but give me time to answer."

"We'll be easy, Sherry. I understand your pain." I looked at Trapper and he smiled. "How well would you say you knew Lisa?"

"As I said, we talked a lot when it was slow. We talked about everything. She told me all about why she moved to Vegas and how she was feeling lonely here."

"Lonely? As in not having male companionship?" Trapper asked.

"Yeah, that. She said she was a loving person and she needed someone to fulfill her." Sherry looked a little embarrassed.

"Are you talking sex? Sorry to be so blunt," I said.

"That's all right. She was very blunt herself, which would embarrass me. But I listened to her and took what she said in stride."

"Did she say anything about how she would fulfill that urge?" I asked.

Sherry was looking more than just embarrassed now. She was turning red as I said, "I'm sorry, Sherry. But we need to know everything. It may help us to find her killer."

"Lisa was very open about her desire to meet men and what she'd do with them. I've never thought about such things, but she had a fixation on sex. That was one of the reasons her boyfriend left her. She said he couldn't perform like she wanted him to. I hate to say it but I believe she had a sex addiction."

"Did she say where she would find men?"

"She mentioned a couple nightclubs and there were a couple of those dating places that find you a date. I'm surprised she just didn't call a male escort service."

Lonely Hearts Murders

"Escort services cost money. Picking up a stranger in a bar is cheaper, but more dangerous. As I'm sure Lisa found out," I probably shouldn't have said that, Sherry flinched. "Did she say what dating services she tried?'

"She mentioned one, 'Love Links', which I think is an online service."

"Sounds like a sex line," Trapper said. "Did Lisa say if she found anyone on this service?"

"She said she had two encounters. Neither one was what she wanted. So she went to another service. I don't know the name of that one."

"I think we can find it. This is very helpful, thank you. Anything else that you think can help?"

"She did say that she thought she had a stalker, but couldn't prove it. She found flowers on her doorstep and a box of candy appeared there also. There were no notes, and she felt that someone was watching her."

I looked at Trapper and said, "Stalkers are good for murder. Too bad she didn't report it."

"Not that LVPD could or would do anything about it. Not until the stalker broke in, then it would be too late," Trapper added.

We thanked Sherry and asked if anyone else on staff would have some information.

"Sure, Lisa was friendly with everyone. I can go get Kathy Jones to talk to you. She and Lisa got along well."

"That would be great. We won't keep her from her duties very long," I said.

"I can have others cover for her," she said and stood.

She went out of the room as Trapper said, "I think it was a date gone bad."

Lonely Hearts Murders

"We know when she was murdered, if we can find out who that date was, we have a start," I said, then paused. "But why would a date shoot her? Strangulation would have been easier and less messy. We'd have to find out if she had sex just before her death. Maybe she found a nutcase and complained that he was lousy in bed."

"Hell, if that was the situation, I would have shot a lot of women," Trapper laughed.

"Yes, but you aren't a nutcase. Or you never let on that you were," I said with a grin.

"I'm very secretive. I have a strange life that I keep to myself," Trapper said.

"I can believe that. I'm going to call Deacon and see if he talked to Greg yet," I said and pulled out my cell phone. I dialed Deacon and waited.

He answered and said, "I'm in the precinct, Jim. I'll talk to you later." Then he hung up.

"I guess he can't talk right now. I'll call later," I said and put my cell phone way.

The door opened and a girl stuck her head in and looked at us.

"Kathy, please came in," I said gently, so not to scare her.

She came over to us and looked uncomfortable. "Please sit, we won't bite."

She sat and said, "Thank you Mr. Richards. I do want to help find the bastard who killed Lisa."

**

Chapter 5

"That's what we want, Kathy. To find the killer. Now just relax and we'll ask you a few questions," I said, softly, seeing she was frightened.

She looked at me and then Trapper. "I do want you to find her killer. If I can help, please ask your questions."

"Good, take a deep breath and relax. Now, you talked a lot to Lisa?" I asked.

"We got along good. Mostly since we worked the same area in the restaurant. Carol was her friend too, but Carol was always in the kitchen, so she didn't get to talk to her very much."

"What things did you talk about?"

"Lots of woman things, personal and professional," she said then paused, looking very upset.

"Is there something you want to tell us, but aren't sure?" I asked.

"Mr. Richards, I don't want to mar the memory of Lisa, but she told me something that she made me promise never to mention to anyone. But I supposed it's moot now that she's gone." She sat back and I could see tears starting to form in her eyes.

"Take your time, we'll wait," I said.

She leaned forward, wiping her eyes, and said, "Lisa told me she was offered a job at an escort service. It would involve her having sex with customers. I knew she didn't mind sex, she actually enjoyed it. But I was afraid for her working for those kind of people. Escort services are no better than a pimp on the streets." She looked annoyed now, almost mad. "I told her she shouldn't get involved with them, but she said the money and benefits were good."

Lonely Hearts Murders

"Do you know the name of the escort service?" Trapper asked.

"She never mentioned it. I never asked. I really didn't want to know what she was getting involved in. I only knew her for a couple months, but I liked her. I didn't know her well enough to tell her what she should and shouldn't do with her life."

"It's not like you were the best of friends, right?" I offered.

"That's right, we weren't. I enjoyed listening to her but from what she told me, I would have never gone out to a bar with her. I'd be concerned that she and I would meet the wrong kind of people."

I thought that was a little late for Lisa. "Did she mention any names of men she knew in the city?"

"No specific names, but she did say she had met a few. From what I got she just used them and dropped them. As I think more about it, she wasn't a very nice girl." Kathy straightened up and looked relieved. "Yes, not a good girl at all. Certainly not someone I would want to associate with," she said and paused. "If you don't have any more questions, I'd like to get back to my area."

"Certainly, Kathy. You've been a big help. Thanks," I said and stood, helping her up. She went to the door and out. I turned to Trapper and said, "Well, it's sounding a little perverted. She made someone mad enough to kill her. Whether it was a customer for sex, or an angry pimp."

Trapper stood and said, "There are dozens of escort services around Vegas. Most are legit providing businessmen with a good looking woman to show off while in town. Then there are those that provide that little extra service for men. Those are still more in number than we have time to track down."

"It's too bad Lisa didn't confide in her co-workers about what the company was called," I said.

"Maybe Deacon did a little exploring around his old precinct. If Greg confided in him, we may have a few more answers," Trapper said.

"I'd really like to get into Lisa's apartment to see if we can find anything connecting her to this escort service. We'll wait until the heat dies down and then take a stroll through the place." I went to the door and out, followed by Trapper.

I stopped at the entrance to tell Sherry, "Thanks, we have enough for now. Tell Angelo we were here and missed him." She smiled as we left the building and went back to the car.

"Where now, chief?" Trapper asked.

"I don't know. We don't have much to go on without seeing what LVPD has on the body. I hope Deacon was more successful than we were." I started the car and drove back to the office.

Penny was sitting with Lacey and Willy when I entered the front. "Sweetie, have you found the killer yet?"

I stared at her. "Your first words to me every time I see you, are asking if I found a killer yet. I appreciate your faith in me, but I don't always have good news." I went by them heading to Deacon's office hoping he was in. He wasn't. "Damn, I hate waiting," I said to myself and went through the back to my office.

I sat at my desk as Willy came barreling in and up to my leg. I picked him up and put him on my desk. Penny followed shortly after, as I figured she would. She sat and gave me a look.

"What did I do now?" I asked.

"Nothing, I'm just amazed that you still look like you did when we first ran into each other," she replied.

"You mean in high school?"

"Oh, hell no. You don't look that good. I mean in 2009, when you came to my rescue from the killers who were taking out cheerleaders. You still look as good as then. What's your secret?"

"Good living, good sex and lots of beer," I joked. "Did you know that the slaves who built the pyramids in Egypt were paid with clay jars of beer? It's true. The pilgrims also had plenty of beer aboard, because it was nutritious and water wasn't drinkable without boiling. No sense burning their boat down boiling water."

"You're making that up," she replied.

"No, I saw it on a history channel program about how beer saved the world. We owe modern medicine, agriculture, the production line to beer and more. I recorded the show, I'll run it for you."

"Some time later. Now, what have you found out about the murder of Carol's friend?"

"Well, it turns out she wasn't a good girl. Not in the sense of good morals."

"In what sense was she not good?"

"Well, she had a sex addiction and was going to work for an escort service. Her co-workers at Angelo's said she enjoyed sex. Even more than you do."

"I beg your pardon. I don't enjoy sex, I just put up with it to keep you happy. I can do without it," she said defiantly.

"Okay, I'll stop, if you stop."

She thought on that. "Maybe later. I'm feeling frisky now that you talked about it."

"Shall we lock the door and put a sock on the doorknob?" I said with a grin.

"I don't think so. I prefer our bedroom. Later," she said and stood. She lifted Willy and said, "I'll see you at home."

Lonely Hearts Murders

She left the room and I sat back wondering why I put up with her. Not that it was bad, no, I enjoyed our times together. She was fun and made my life what it is, beautiful. But then I thought about the dead girl and wondered what was wrong with this world.

If it weren't for crime and people doing bad things, I'd be out of business. The police would have to do traffic duty and helping old ladies across the streets, it wouldn't be the mess it is today.

**

Chapter 6

I was deep in thought when I heard someone approaching my door. It was Deacon, followed by Trapper.

"About time," I said, standing. "Sit and talk to me."

They came in and sat in the client chairs. Deacon cleared his throat and said, "I went to the precinct and found Captain Weber talking to Greg in the squad room. Weber was happy to see me and invited me and Greg into his office. We sat and Weber asked me all about how I was doing. I kept my answers to a minimum and hoped they would talk about the murder. Weber asked what I was doing there and I told him I came by to say hi to everyone. Okay, I lied a little, but it was partly true."

"So, did they talk about the murder?" I asked impatiently.

Lonely Hearts Murders

"Weber finally asked Greg how his case was going. I just listened to what Greg said, he wasn't paying attention to my being there. I guess he figured if it was alright with Weber, he would talk about it in front of me."

"Okay, so what was said?"

"The girl was murdered in her apartment, in the bedroom. Shot in the back of the head while on the bed, face down. They figured that out by the blood splatter. There were no defensive wounds so she didn't fight and she did have sex just before her death. They are running tox on her to see if she may have been drugged, no word yet. CSI said the room had been wiped clean so the killer may not be identified."

"Maybe they can get DNA from the semen?" Trapper asked.

"The autopsy said there was none. The killer must have worn a condom and taken it with him. To me, this sounds all too professional."

"Yes, it does," I said and looked at Trapper. "Do you think an escort service would hire a hitman to take out the girl?"

"For what purpose? They have no trade secrets or national security issues to protect. Why kill her? I think this was a very clever killer, who didn't want to be caught."

"I'm thinking a serial killer," I said.

"That's what Greg said," Deacon added. "He felt it was the same M.O. as one other case they had from last year. Girl shot in the back of the head, in bed, and dumped behind the Monte Carlo hotel parking structure. Greg said they should call him the casino killer. Weber didn't care for the name. He said it might scare people away from the casinos."

"Whatever, it's now a dangerous game for the killer, and there could be more. We need to know if the other victim from last year was part of an escort service."

"She was a hooker, from what Greg said. She had been arrested a number of times previous. Keller didn't have any priors for prostitution. Greg said that was the only difference."

"Let's fill Greg in on what we know. It may help to find the escort service our vic worked for."

"Your vic worked for an escort service? I thought she worked for Angelo?" Deacon asked.

"From what the co-workers at the restaurant told us, she started working for one recently. She also had a sex addiction." I told Deacon.

"Most hookers aren't addicted to sex. It's all for love of a pimp, drugs, or the money. Depending on how they are soliciting," Trapper said.

"We know with our vic, it was for the sex. She may have been unfortunately picked by the killer because she came from the escort service. But if she did, then the service would have a record of the person who hired her. We do have to bring Greg in on this."

"I'll call him and have him come in to talk," Deacon said and pulled his cell phone. He stood and went out in the hallway for privacy.

"It may help us and give Greg credit for breaking the case," I said.

"I hope you're right," Trapper added.

We waited for Deacon to come back. He finally walked in and said, "Greg is on his way."

"Good, let's go to the break room and hit the new food machines I had installed," I said.

"You had food machines put in? When?" Trapper asked.

"Two days ago. You've been away on a case following a spouse."

"What kind of machines?" he asked.

"Two machines, candy in one, and the other smaller one has sandwiches and canned soup." I stood and they followed me to the break room.

We sat after making our selections in the machine. I got a tuna sandwich that wasn't bad. "They check the machines three times a week. So everything is fresh."

Lacey came in the room and went to the candy machine. She glanced at us as she pulled the knob for a candy bar, and said, "No work today?"

"We're waiting for Greg Warren to come in for a talk. When he gets here send him in," I said.

"In here?" she asked.

"No, my office. We should be in there shortly."

She acknowledged and left.

We sat munching, then Deacon spoke, "Greg is a pretty sharp guy. He has a good head for deducing things. If we share with him, he may share with us. We work together, we may have this solved."

"I hope so. I told Carol that I would find the killer and I don't want to disappoint her."

"I wonder if Carol knew about the vic's love of sex?" Trapper asked.

"I don't know, but I'll ask her. Shall we go back to my office and wait for Greg?"

We stood and went out into the hallway. We arrived at my office door just as Greg entered from the front. "Hey, Greg. Perfect timing. Come on in," I said as we all went in.

We sat as Greg said, "Deacon told me you have some information on the Keller murder?"

"We do. I promised my daughter that I would help find the killer. So we did a little investigating earlier. We talked to the girls that work at Angelo's, where Keller worked."

"She worked for Angelo. I didn't know that," Greg said with a frown.

"It would have eventually come to you. Anyway, we think Keller was playing a dangerous game with an escort service." I told Greg everything we learned from the waitresses. He sat nodding as I finished.

"Well, this helps. It's too bad they didn't know what escort service she worked for. I'll have some of the detectives go hit up a couple of the less reputable ones. Maybe we'll get lucky and find the one she worked for. Thanks, guys, this helps."

"Any word on promotions?" I asked.

"After Deacon left, Weber told me that it was looking good for me to take the squad as lieutenant. I'm happy about that."

"Well, we're happy for you. You deserve it," Deacon said.

"Besides, you need a friendly face on the LVPD to help with your cases," Greg joked.

"With Lynn and Deacon gone, you're our only connection, besides Weber. You know he won't help us," I said.

"Weber has mellowed a bit, now that he's retiring soon."

"Really? When?" Trapper asked.

"He's talking about two months, when his anniversary of forty years on the force comes up."

I was surprised, "Forty years? He must have seen a lot of crime in that time."

**

Chapter 7

"He has. But now his reign of terror is going to end. I like the man, although he's a bit odd, and I hope they get someone to replace him who's a little more efficient," Greg said.

"I put up with him all those years I was on the force," Trapper said. "But we made our peace."

"Okay, so I need to get on the escort services. I'll call you if we have anything of interest." Greg stood and thanked us again and then left.

"He's going to do a lot of leg work, chasing down all the escort services in Vegas. But he has his men to do most of that. So, what do we do now?" Trapper said.

"Find us a serial killer. Maybe I need to talk to Angelo and see if we can get some men on the streets, too," I said with a big grin.

Trapper laughed and said, "I'm sure the mob will frighten the people at an escort service a lot faster than the cops. They know cops are bound by laws, but the mob has its own laws and they aren't pleasant."

"Exactly. Shall we go get some muscle?"

"Do you mind if I take off?" Deacon said. "I'd like to take my daughter and Lynn to get some ice cream. I did promise them,"

"Go ahead, Will and I can handle this," I replied.

"Thanks," Deacon said and left the room.

I stood and said, "I don't know if Angelo is back from visiting his new girlfriend. It's getting late and I have a horny woman at home," I said with a grin. "We can start fresh in the morning."

Lonely Hearts Murders

"Sounds like a plan. I need to see Samantha, I've neglected her lately."

"Okay, we'll head out first thing in the morning."

We both went out of my office, Trapper went back to his office and I went to the lobby. Lacey was at her desk and looked up when I came through the glass doors.

"Are you coming up to bother me?" she asked quickly.

"No, I came up to tell you to go get Tracy in the outer lobby and lock up. Then go home to your family. I'm sure Jessie will still be happy about her birthday party."

"Did you see the look on her face? I never knew exactly when she was born, so Mac did some detective work and got hold of her birth certificate at the county building. After her father was murdered and we took her in as foster parents, I felt bad that we never celebrated her birthday properly. Once a year we would take her out to dinner, give her a few presents and that was it. She never had a fancy party like we threw her."

"She's a young girl and needs things like that, especially knowing when exactly she was born. You should find out who her friends are and have a party with them."

"That's good, I'll do that. Thanks." She stood and grabbed her purse, then went out the front doors to the outer lobby. I watched her talking to Tracy and they both went out the front entrance. I hoped Lacey remembered to lock the door.

I went back into the hallway and saw Fred our handyman and night watchman coming in the back door. He smiled when he saw me and stood waiting. I went to him and said, "Hey, Fred, what's up?"

"I just took Henry to the vet, he was feeling a little under the weather. The vet gave him a shot and pills that I have to get down his throat."

Lonely Hearts Murders

"Willy gets sick every so often, usually from eating the wrong thing. Maybe Henry found something outside that he ate."

"Anything is possible. But he seems better now."

"I'm glad. Well, everyone is leaving. I think Buck and Earl are off on a case, I haven't seen them since earlier. So, the building is all yours. You aren't getting bored with this job are you?"

"Oh, gosh no. I enjoy working with everyone and working in the flower gardens. I would never leave here."

"Good. I have to get home, my wife is expecting me. Take care." I went past him and out the back door. Henry was in the dog run on the side of the building and sat watching me. I waved to him and went to my car.

I arrived home a short time later and parked in the garage. I went around the side of the garage to check on my motorhome, wishing we could go traveling one more time. I went in the house and it was quiet.

I didn't call out for Penny, because I had a feeling where she was, in the bedroom. Unfortunately she was sleeping when I got there. I stood at the door watching her softly breathing and smiled. I went back to the living room and sat in front of the TV when Willy came slowly walking out from the hallway. I helped him up on the couch and we sat watching the news.

I didn't really like watching the news, but today was different. I felt I had to watch. They reported on a few minor crimes in Las Vegas and traffic on the Strip. Then a report came on about a fire in a local business. The Vegas Escort Service. That caught my attention and I turned up the volume. Seems the fire started about two hours ago and most of the building was destroyed.

"Well, that's one we won't be able to question," I said to Willy.

Lonely Hearts Murders

"What one?" came a sleepy voice from the hallway. It was Penny.

"I'm sorry, did I wake you with the TV?"

"No, I was having a dream that you were dating a brunette, and I shot her," she said and sat next to me.

"Well, that wasn't nice."

"I should have shot you for dating her. But I didn't. I don't know what was wrong with me."

"You love me too much," I replied and kissed her on the cheek. "Now, do you want to do what you said in my office? A little roll in the bed?"

"Are you kidding? After you cheated on me?" She gave me her icy stare and I didn't say anything more.

We watched the TV for a short while, then went to the bedroom. She was now feeling frisky. It was an interesting evening.

"Did you forgive me my indiscretion with the brunette?" I said as we rested.

"No, but I like using you. Now if I find you out with a blonde, you are really in trouble, mister." She turned on her side, away from me and went to sleep.

After a short while, she was softly snoring again. So I got up, took my cell phone, went to the kitchen and took a beer out of the fridge. I went back to the living room and sat, turning on the TV, with no sound. I watched the screen as I dialed Trapper.

He came on and said, "Did you see the news?"

"I did. It's a strange coincidence. I wonder if it's the place Keller worked out of. We need to get into her apartment and search."

"It's dark out, we wouldn't be seen easily. Shall we go now?"

"Aren't you with Sam?"

"I am, but she fell asleep," he said laughing.

"What's wrong with our women?" I asked.

**

Chapter 8

"Let's meet at the office and we'll go from there." Trapper agreed and I hung up. I went into the bedroom and took out some dark clothes. I told Willy to watch mommy, left her a note that I was going out with a blonde. That should give her something to fuss over.

I went out to the car and drove to the office. I pulled into the back and saw Trapper's Jeep. He had to be inside, so I went in. I found Trapper sitting with Fred in the break room.

"Are you comfortable?" I asked.

"Sure. Are you ready to go?" he replied.

I sighed, turned and went to the back door. Trapper laughed and followed. We went to my car and I drove back to the apartment where Keller lived.

We arrived at the apartment and went to the door.

"You're the expert at picking locks," I said to Trapper.

"Just so happens I have my tools with me," he grinned and proceeded to pick the lock. The door opened and we ducked under the police tape going in. The place was dark and we didn't want any light to be seen, so we used our flashlights carefully.

Lonely Hearts Murders

I went to a desk with papers on the top in a mess. I hoped maybe we would find a pay stub from the service, although I figured they paid under the table. I went through the papers, mostly bills and credit card receipts. She had expensive tastes in clothing, according to the store receipts. I finally found a handwritten note saying 'Vegas Escort, two pm Thursday' and that was all. I figured that was where she was going for her new job and it was the place that burned down.

Trapper was rummaging around the bedroom and called to me softly. I went to see him and found a grisly scene. Blood was splattered on the walls and the bed's headboard. The pillow and sheets were missing, probably taken by CSI. There was a blood soaked spot on the bed.

"Evidently, the killer let her bleed out for a while before he moved her. Probably didn't want too much blood in his car," Trapper said.

"Nothing was said if her body was found wrapped in plastic or just dropped off as was," I added.

"If she was dropped off as was, I wonder if she had clothing on. Deacon said that she had sex just before she was murdered. The ultimate insult, dropping her naked," Trapper said.

"I found a note that I presume she wrote about the Vegas Escort Service. I think she was going there, probably for a job interview."

"Most of those places don't hire women through interviews. They recruit them off the streets or from referrals. Hooking isn't a college course that a person would put on their resume," he replied.

"True, but she was going there for something. Now the place is gone, so we can't check on who hired her," I said.

"Maybe the killer torched the place to hide his identity," Trapper offered.

"I think he would have used an alias when he went to hire an escort."

"True, I don't think he was that stupid. Especially since he wiped this place clean after he murdered her."

"Let's get out of here, I got one piece of info about the escort service."

"I'm right behind you," Trapper said and went ahead of me.

"You are such a smart-ass," I said and followed.

We locked the door and went to the car. I sat looking at the note about the Vegas Escort Service. "It was something she wanted to remember, so she wrote it down."

I started the car and dropped Trapper off at his Jeep. "See you in the morning and we'll pick Greg's brain for information on the fire." He agreed and went to his vehicle.

Bob Moats

I drove back home wondering if Penny got my note. I hope she thought it was supposed to be funny. But then I should prepare myself for whatever she does.

I parked the car for the night and went in through the kitchen. I was greeted with a face full of water. Penny was standing in the kitchen with a water pistol in her hand.

"I told you I'd shoot you if you went out with a blonde," she laughed and ran out of the kitchen. I went to get a paper towel to wipe my face and glasses.

I looked down at Willy and said, "You could have warned me."

She had already undressed as I went into the bedroom and told her about Trapper and me going to the apartment. I didn't get into graphic detail about the bedroom, just the minor details.

She sat up in bed as I talked and took off my clothes. Willy was sitting next to her watching me also. I slipped under the covers and said, "Good night."

She kissed me and turned on her side. She was asleep in minutes. It always amazed me how fast she could go out. I take forever drifting off to sleep. My mind wanders too much and I need to make it go blank. But that was easier said than done. I was thinking about why someone would burn down the escort service that Lisa may have worked for. Were they afraid of being found out? I doubted that, but it was a logical reason, if the killer used his own name, which I doubted.

I finally fell asleep.

The next morning I heard Penny rummaging about in her bathroom just off the bedroom. My bathroom was down the hall and I stumbled to it. I did like having my own bathroom, for obvious reasons. My farts didn't have a rosy scent. I shaved and showered then went back to the bedroom to dress. Penny was gone.

Bob Moats

I went out to the kitchen just as Penny was leaving to go to her TV studio to tape her show. "Who's on the show today?" I asked.

"Some TV show cast, all six of them. They're in Vegas to shoot an episode. I get to interview them."

"Any show that I might know?"

"It's a new show that isn't starting until fall, so you wouldn't know it."

"Okay, I'll set the DVR to record your show. Be careful on the roads." I kissed her and she went out taking Willy with her.

I put bread in the toaster and waited for it to burn. I ate and got my things ready to go to the office. I set the DVR to record Penny's show and went out to the car.

I arrived at the office and could tell by their cars parked in the lot that everyone was in. I went in and up to the front where Lacey was talking to Lynn. They both turned to me when I came through the glass doors.

Lonely Hearts Murders

"Good morning, is everyone ready for the day?" I said.

I looked over to the waiting area and saw a woman sitting on the couch. Lacey stood from her desk and came to the counter where I was now standing.

"Jim, this woman wants to talk to you," Lacey said quietly. I thanked her and went to the woman.

"I'm Jim Richards. I understand you want to talk to me?" I said to her.

As she stood, I could see she was thin, and barely five-foot-two, by my estimates. She smiled and said, "Thanks, Mr. Richards. I'm Sue Hanson, bounty hunter."

**

Chapter 9

I was taken aback by her comment. This diminutive woman, looking barely 110 pounds wet, came up to between my belt and my chest, was a bounty hunter? Was someone pulling a joke on me? She was a brunette, so it wouldn't be Penny, she would have sent a blonde.

"Well, nice to meet you. Won't you follow me to my office?" I said, turning and holding the glass doors open for her. She breezed through and I had to move quickly to keep up. I called to her, giving directions. She went in my office and I followed.

"Please have a seat," I said and went around to my desk and sat. She sat up properly and smiled.

"Now you wanted to talk to me, why?"

Lonely Hearts Murders

"I was told you could help. I just came in from Michigan and talked to a cop there named Becker. He said if I came here to look you up, he said you could introduce me to the right people."

I realized she was talking about Barry Becker, who I knew from the Clinton Township police back in Michigan. It was where Trapper was a lieutenant and Becker's boss. I smiled thinking that our paths crossed over two thousand miles away.

"What is it you need?"

"I'm chasing a man who was reported to have come here. Barry Becker said you know people in the LVPD so I could get help in finding him."

"Well, there is one of my associates who could help you better. He was Becker's boss back in Michigan and he worked here in Vegas as a cop years ago. So he knows many of the right people who can help you. I'll go get him and have you two talk about your problem."

I stood and excused myself. I went to Trapper's office. He looked up from the newspaper he was reading. "Seems the entire escort building was razed. The paper said it looked like an arsonist was behind it. Unconfirmed sources say someone tossed in a couple Molotov cocktails through the windows and set the place on fire."

"Well, we can mark that one off our imaginary list," I said. "I have another problem for you in my office."

"Oh, what kind?" he asked.

"A woman. Interested?" I grinned.

He jumped up and said, "Lead the way."

He followed me back to my office and we went in. I went to my desk as Trapper stood just in the doorway.

"Will, this is Sue Hanson, bounty hunter. Sue, this is Will Trapper, formerly of the

Clinton Township police and the LVPD, now one of the investigators here."

Trapper went to her and held his hand out. She took it and smiled. "I understand you've worked with Barry Becker?"

He looked surprised and said, "Yes, I have, he's a fine officer. You know him?"

"Only in passing. I was in his precinct looking for a man who skipped his court hearing and heard he was last in Clinton Township. Becker helped, but found out the man fled to Las Vegas. Becker told me to look up Jim Richards when I got here. So, here I am."

Trapper sat in the chair next to her and asked, "Can you fill me in a little more on the man you're hunting?"

"He was arrested on suspicion of murdering a woman in Missouri, shooting her in the head while she was in bed."

Trapper looked at me when she mentioned the shooting of the woman. I thought it sounded familiar to the shooting of our victim.

She continued, "He was going to trial for it but he fled to Michigan and I tracked him to Clinton Township where he had a cousin. As I said he left Michigan for Vegas last week and I'm here to find him."

"Do you know why he came here?" I asked.

"I understand from his cousin that he used to live here, but left a year ago. He has friends here who are probably hiding him."

I looked at Trapper and said, "He was here a year ago, when that hooker was shot in the head, then goes to Missouri where he commits the same crime, then comes here and shoots Keller. I think he may be our man."

I could see the confusion on Sue's face. I said, "I'm sorry, but we have a case of murder similar to what your man did. We believe he's a serial killer. What's his name?"

"George Conner," she said. "Although he's used other aliases. Conner is his real name."

"I know just the LVPD detective who would be interested in your story," Trapper said. "He's assigned to the murder we just had recently. I'll call him and have him come to talk to you."

"Thank you, Mr. Trapper. I'll need to find a motel in which to stay, so shall I wait here until he comes?"

"Let me see if he can come in right away, I'll call now." Trapper took out his cell phone and speed dialed Greg. Trapper explained briefly what we had and then hung up. "He said he'll be right over. After you're done with him, I can take you to a nice motel and you can get yourself settled. I do believe it will be a few days before Conner will surface." Trapper looked at me and said,

"Let's take Sue to our break room and get her a refreshment."

I stood, as did Trapper. I could see the look of surprise on his face when Sue stood. I don't think he was ready to see such a smallish woman tracking a cold-blooded killer.

She saw his expression, smiled and said, "Yes, I'm small, but I'm tough. At the gun shop where I buy my weapons, they call me 'Trouble' and I am. Now you have any good soda pop in your break room?"

Trapper grinned and said to follow him. I said I was going to wait for Greg and they left my office. I thought on this situation, amazed that this information dropped on our laps was coming from our old stomping grounds back in Michigan. So, Conner lived in Vegas last year, and disappeared after the murder of the girl here. Then he was involved in a murder in Missouri, same M.O., then on to Vegas where another girl was killed the same way. Three deaths and he seems connected to them.

Lonely Hearts Murders

I went out to the lobby to wait for Greg. Lacey and Lynn were there talking, but before I could talk to them, Greg Warren came into the building. He said hello to everyone and said to me, "I'm hoping you have some more information. The fire at the Vegas Escort building was deliberate, I think it may have had to do with the vic."

"It seems there's another investigation paralleling ours. There's a bounty hunter here looking for a man who had committed similar crimes. Could be a good lead on our case. Sorry, your case."

"Jim, you know I do depend on your help, so it's our case," Greg said just as Trapper and Sue came out to the lobby.

Greg turned to them and made a strange expression that I could see. "Something wrong, Greg?" I asked.

He smiled and said, "Sue?"

She gave him a strange look also. "Greg, is that you?"

"It's me," he replied.

"Okay, you know each other, how?" I asked.

Greg looked at me and said, "I'm from Missouri, where I grew up with Sue. We were going steady in high school."

**

Chapter 10

I think Trapper and I were both surprised to hear that. Sue and Greg went to each other and hugged. They broke away and Greg said, "How have you been?"

"Good. I never thought you'd end up a cop, least of all a detective. Congratulations," she replied.

Lonely Hearts Murders

"And you're a bounty hunter? That's a job I never thought you'd be doing. So, Jim told me you are looking for a felon who may be connected to a couple murders here in Vegas."

"Let's all go in my office and relax while you two talk." I went to the door as I looked back to Lacey and Lynn. They were watching us go. I told Trapper to take them to my office and went to Lynn.

"Did you have a nice time getting ice cream with Deacon?" I asked her.

"We did. Then we went to Circus, Circus to wander around. Little Penny is starting to understand what's going on around her," Lynn said with pride.

"She'll grow up fast, so enjoy her now. We'll talk later." I turned and went back to my office and sat at my desk.

Sue and Greg were reminiscing about their lives after high school. I sat waiting for them to come back to the present. Greg looked at Trapper and me and apologized.

"Sorry guys, it's been a long time. My family moved from Missouri to Vegas after I was out of school, so we lost connection." He looked to Sue and said, "So, tell me everything about your man."

Sue went back over the timeline of her case, as Greg was listening.

"I do see a pattern there. So your killer could be our killer. Do you have any information as to where he could be?"

"Not really, other than he may be staying with a couple of people here in Vegas that he knew. His cousin in Michigan gave me a few names that might help."

"If you could write down those names, I can have them looked up and we can go see if Conner is with one of them." Greg said.

She agreed and asked me for a pad and pen. I gave her mine and she took out a small notebook from her purse and copied down the names on my pad. "I'm giving you my fugitive info, since you think he committed a murder here recently. But he's a fugitive from Missouri and they may want him back. I'll let you fight with them over jurisdiction."

"I'm sure we can come to an agreement. Do you make any money if you bring him back?" Greg asked.

"My bail bonds agent is interested in him being brought back. He put up a lot of money for Conner. I get a percentage of the bail if I turn him in."

"We'll work something out. If you catch him and turn him over to the police, you've fulfilled your obligation. Even if it's not the police in Missouri. Then it's our problem to turn him over to the proper agency."

"Thank you, Greg. I appreciate that." She finished writing and handed the pad to Greg. He tore off the top sheet and gave the pad back to me.

"I'll get this to my men and have them follow up on Conner," Greg said and looked at Sue, "Where are you staying?"

"Nowhere yet. Mr. Trapper said he would help me find a motel," she replied.

Greg looked at Trapper. "I'll get her settled, thanks, Will." He stood and helped Sue up. Trapper and I stood as Greg led her out of the room.

"I bet that Greg will put her up in his apartment," Trapper smiled.

"I'll take that bet. Greg's a decent guy and would never do something like that. He'll find a nice motel and pay for her stay," I smiled.

"It's a bet. Say a hundred dollars? Shall we have Lacey hold the money?" Trapper asked.

"No, I don't trust her with our money. We'll have Earl hold it," I said with a grin.

"Fine, we need to watch Greg and see what he does."

"We need to find the people that Conner knew here in Vegas," I said.

"How? Greg took the list." Trapper said.

"Oh, ye of little faith," I spoke and picked up the pad of paper. I turned the top sheet and took out a sheet of carbon paper. "She wrote on the top sheet that Greg took, but the carbon paper below the next sheet traced everything to the page below it." I turned the pad and showed Trapper the names all written in black on the sheet.

"You are devious. How did you think of that?"

"It's an old trick used by mentalists to get a question written by a person who wants the mentalist to answer."

Trapper smiled and said, "I have my faith in you restored. Where shall we start?"

"Let's take this list to someone who can dig into it."

"Who?" Trapper asked.

"Angelo. His network is huge. He has friends in every corner of Vegas. If anyone can find even one of these names, he can. If we find one, then that person may know the others. Let's go before Conner goes deep into hiding."

"I don't think he knows that he has a small woman chasing after him, so he probably feels safe," Trapper said.

"But if he murdered Keller, he'd have to be careful. As I said, we need to get on this fast." I stood and went out of my office followed by Trapper. I went to the front and told Lacey we were going to be out.

"Good, and stay out," she replied.

"You can be replaced," I laughed.

"Just try it," she retorted back.

Lonely Hearts Murders

I went back to the hallway and out the back door. Trapper was trying to keep up with me. I was moving fast since I wanted to catch this killer for my daughter.

We drove out and over to Mama Mia Restaurant, where I turned over the car to the parking valet. We went in and found Angelo out in the dining room talking to people. The man was a gentle giant in the mob family, but very dangerous if crossed. He was enjoying his role as an owner of the restaurant and meeting and greeting with customers. He looked over and saw us.

He excused himself and came to us. "Mr. R. and Mr. T. good to see youse back. Do you have something for me to help find the murderer?"

"I think we do, can we talk in private?" I said.

"Follow me," he said and went to his office.

We all sat and I handed him the copy of the names from the list. "We have a possible name of the killer, George Conner. These names are where he may be hiding out with a few of his friends in Vegas. We don't have the resources that LVPD has to find these people, but I trust your connections to find them."

"I'm honored that you have that faith in me. I'll do my best to find these mooks," he said, looking serious. "I'll call you when I have something."

"Thanks, Angelo," I said and stood. "We'll wait to hear from you."

"Count on it," Angelo growled.

I motioned to Trapper and we left.

**

Chapter 11

Out in the car I thought about Carol. She was alone, with no boyfriend or husband. I worried about her meeting men and what could happen.

"Where's your mind off to?" Trapper asked as I sat there.

"Huh? Oh, sorry. I was just thinking about my daughter and what kind of men she would meet."

"You should have her tell you who she's seeing and then you can run a check on them," he said with a grin.

"Seriously, I might do that. How many times have we seen murders by serial killers that have gone on for way too long before the killer was caught?" I said.

"Don't forget about all the ones who got away with it. There are a lot of murderers out there who are still wandering the streets. But if you obsess over it, you'll go crazy."

"True, I still have to keep my faith in mankind," I said.

"Your first mistake. Now where are we going to go?"

"Let's go to see Greg and find out what he's got." I started the car and drove over to Greg's precinct. We went in and were greeted by a number of police who knew us. Especially Trapper, since he was a legend around here for his past as a cop. Even if he was a naughty cop, he was admired. How many police precincts can say they had hookers in holding cells and not for arrest? Trapper had a thing for hookers. Not that he indulged in their business, he just had a compassion for them.

"Is Greg Warren nearby?" Trapper asked one officer in the squad room.

"He's in with Weber. I think the old man is going to retire," the officer replied.

We went towards Weber's office and could see Greg in with Weber. I looked over to Greg's desk and saw Sue Hanson sitting at his desk. I tapped Trapper and motioned to her. We went over and she smiled when she saw us.

"Greg's captain wanted to see him, so he had me wait here," she said.

"How long has he been in there?" I asked.

"About twenty minutes, they both look serious. I've been watching."

I looked over and saw them stand. Weber shook Greg's hand and gave him an envelope. They said something and laughed. I hoped that was a good sign. Greg came out of the office followed by Weber. The Captain stood in the squad room and looked around.

"Give me your attention over here," he yelled loudly. Everyone shut up and watched the man. "I have an announcement to make. Paperwork just came through to appoint Greg Warren as a new lieutenant."

Everyone cheered and whooped it up. Weber yelled for silence.

"We can celebrate later, crime doesn't stop for good news. Now I have another announcement. I know it's been rumored that I'm retiring in a couple months." More cheering broke out. "Shut it," Weber yelled and smiled. "I hate to make everyone wait, so I put in for an early retirement this morning. I'll be leaving by this weekend."

Nobody cheered, they were all stunned.

"I'm going to be replaced by a new captain, who just got her promotion." Weber smiled.

I thought I heard him right, he said "her."

Lonely Hearts Murders

"That's right, your new captain will be a woman, Lorelei Paris. You all know her, she's worked out of this precinct a couple times. I think she'll do well if you bozos don't give her a hard time."

Everyone laughed, I was stunned. I've worked with Lorelei a couple times on cases. I had to try to keep Penny from thinking we were having an affair. She was one hot woman, and could be a distraction. But I believed she could handle it.

"So men," Weber went on, "you will give her the respect you gave me. Actually I should say give her the respect you never gave me."

Everyone laughed again. "I'm going to miss all you flatfoots. We had a good run, and I will be coming in often to see how you're behaving," he said with a slight choke in his voice. "Now get to work, there's crime to solve," he said and turned quickly going out of the room.

"Wow," Trapper said and excused himself. He went after Weber, I could tell. They had a history together and I'm sure Trapper was going to have a talk with him. Greg came over to Sue and me and was looking flushed.

"Are you going to be okay?" I asked him.

"This is a real surprise. I'm just trying to absorb it all. I'll be alright shortly," he said with a grin.

"Okay, Lieutenant Warren, have you found any of the men Conner could be living with?"

"No, we just got here when Weber called me. I'll have to have one of my men check the names. Listen to me, 'my men,' isn't that nice?"

"Don't get a big head now. They can give you a hard time," I said. "Time is wasting and Conner is either going on a killing spree or going deep undercover."

Lonely Hearts Murders

"You're right," he said and turned to Williams, "Bernie, can you come here?"

Williams came over and Greg showed him the list. "Get someone to help locating these men. Then when you have the addresses, get back to me."

Williams went back to his desk and called one other detective to help him.

Greg turned to me and said, "Everything is happening so fast. My promotion and Weber retiring. I may need to absorb all this for a day or two."

"Don't let this keep you from finding the killer. I promised my daughter I would find him. With your help or without. I'm not resting until he's locked up in jail." I looked to Sue and said, "I'll help you find him, can you handle him?"

"I may look small and weak, but don't mess with me," she said with a wry smile.

"Jim, I understand what you are going through with Carol, but please leave this to the police," Greg said.

I smiled and said, "Greg, I'm very happy for you. I hope all goes well. Sue it was nice meeting you, have faith in Greg, he'll get you your man, if I don't." I turned and went to the hallway where Weber and Trapper disappeared to. I found them in the captain's office laughing.

"Jim," Weber called to me. "Come over and join us."

I went and sat. "So, you're going to retire? What are you going to do?"

"I have a small cabin up by Reno. I will be going there to relax. If I can leave the wife here," he laughed and sat back. "Seriously, I may take a month to get used to the idea of not chasing criminals and putting up with unruly cops. I've really enjoyed you sticking your nose in and helping with our past crimes. You have helped us. I hope you can help Lorelei when she takes over. I know you've worked with her."

"I have and she is a great detective. I'm sure she'll be a great captain in your place," I said.

"So, give her your best. Just don't tell Penny about it," he laughed.

**

Chapter 12

I laughed and thought about Penny's reaction to Lorelei being the new captain. Penny wasn't really a jealous woman, she knew I'd never stray. And at great risk to my life I never would.

"So when is this transition going to take place?" I asked.

"This weekend. Friday she comes in to get organized with my help and Monday I'm gone. I'll probably come in over the weekend to clean out my office," Weber said.

"If you need help, let me know," Trapper offered.

"Sure, help get me out fast," Weber laughed.

"I'm going to miss you, Captain. Really," Trapper said with a slight choke. "We've been through a lot. I still enjoy thinking about all those pranks Becker and I pulled on you when we came out for Jim and Penny's wedding."

"Yeah, and the look on your face when you thought those fake FBI men were going to arrest you. My favorite prank on you."

Trapper cracked a smile as my cell phone buzzed. I excused myself and went out to the hallway. Caller ID said it was Angelo. I hoped he had good news. "Hey, Angelo, have you got something for me?"

"I got two of the names and locations, we're working on the rest. Do you want to write these down?"

"Go ahead and read them, my phone records when I push a button." Which I did.

He read the names he had and I thanked him. "I'll see about the other two and get back to you."

"Thanks, I hope we can find the man at one of these locations. I'll wait on your call," I said and hung up. I went back into Weber's office and asked, "Captain, do you have a piece of paper?"

He opened a drawer on his desk and pulled out a sheet, handing it to me.

I sat in a corner of the room and ran the recording of Angelo's addresses. I wrote them down. Trapper was watching me and asked, "Whatcha got?"

"A couple of addresses from Angelo. Feel like taking a ride?" I asked.

He looked at Weber, "Duty calls. Let me know if you need help moving?"

"I will, thanks," he replied, looking serious.

Trapper stood and followed me down the hallway. We passed Greg and Sue, still at Greg's desk. I waved to them and kept going.

"Did Angelo find all of them?" Trapper asked.

"Just two, he said he'd call with the others. This will be a good start. Maybe we'll get lucky and find him in one of these addresses."

"The guy is a serial killer, do you think he'll want to be found?"

"He may be dumb enough to relax at one," I replied.

Lonely Hearts Murders

"Are you armed?" Trapper asked me.

"Of course. I never leave home without it. I hope we don't need them, but I'm sure we will."

We got to my car and drove out heading to the first address on West Carey Avenue, near the North Vegas airport. "Maybe he figures he can highjack a plane and escape."

"I'm not chasing planes," Trapper exclaimed with a grin.

"Don't panic, I'm sure we can stop him before he flies off."

"I certainly hope so." Trapper sat back and smiled.

We arrived at the address and I drove past the house. I parked down the street and we looked back. "It looks deserted. No curtains on the windows and no car in the drive. Shall we proceed?" I asked.

"We came all this way, why stop now?" he replied.

"Good. Then let's attack the fort," I said and opened my door. I stepped out and stood. Trapper stood on his side of the car looking at the house.

"It's quiet here, other than the planes taking off from the airport. Shall we go right up to the house or sneak around the back?" Trapper said.

"We'll go to the front door. I'll pretend we are hustling for religion."

"Oh, yes, you are good at that," Trapper said with a sneer.

We walked down the street and up to the house. I could see in the front window that there was little furniture. A couch, easy chair and a coffee table that held what could be described as drug paraphernalia. I said, "If nothing else, we can bust them for drugs."

Lonely Hearts Murders

I knocked on the door and we waited. No one came so I knocked again. I heard a noise in the room and saw someone looking out the window at us. I smiled and waved. The person ducked back in and was gone. I knocked again and this time the door opened a crack.

"What the hell do you want?" he yelled.

"Have you been saved by our lord and savior Jesus?" I yelled back.

"Are you crazy? Go away before I stick your religion up your ass," he yelled back out.

"Okay, let's try this. Is George Conner here?"

I could see the man respond to the question, he seemed startled.

"I know George and if you see him, tell him I'll kill him if he comes around." He slammed the door quickly. I could hear him ranting obscene things about Conner.

"Okay, first address, a bust. Let's hit the next." We turned off the porch and back to the car. I looked at the address and started the car.

We arrived at an apartment building and found the one we needed.

"At least he's not going to fly away," Trapper said.

"Yet," I replied. We got out and went to the apartment number on the list.

"Are you playing the holy card again?" Trapper asked.

"No, I'm just going with the direct approach," I said and knocked on the door. I could hear someone moving about in the apartment, so I waited.

"Someone just peeked out the window," Trapper said.

"We don't look like cops, do we?" I asked just as the door opened. There was an attractive woman standing just inside. I could see she had bruises on her face and arms.

"I didn't call the cops, so what do you want?" she spit out.

"We're not cops. I'm Benjamin Pierce and this is John McIntyre. We are investigators for Global Insurance Corporation. We are trying to track down a man who is a beneficiary of a life insurance policy. It's worth a lot of money and we need to find the person."

She squinted at us. I thought the bruises would hurt if she made a face, but she didn't flinch.

"Who you looking for?" she asked.

"George Conner, we tracked him down to this address. The policy was for a great deal of money and we need to find him to give him a check."

She paused, thinking. "Give it to me, I'll see he gets it."

"Oh, we can't do that. He has to provide ID and sign for the check, just to prove we got the right person."

She paused again. "He's not here right now. He's probably out drinking or whoring around."

"Are you related to him?" I asked.

"Oh, hell, no. He just stays here when he's in town. I stupidly let him stay. If I don't, he'll beat on me."

"Is that how you got all those bruises?" I asked cautiously.

She didn't reply. "Give me your card and I'll call when he returns."

I took out my extra wallet and pulled out one of the four fake cards I had for this type of occasion. I gave it to her and said, "Please call."

**

Chapter 13

She closed the door without further words. Trapper and I smiled at each other, since we were real close now. I turned and went back to the car as Trapper was saying this could go bad.

"Why? He's just a man who likes to murder people. What could go wrong?" I replied.

"Murder is the operative word here. He could kill that girl if she doesn't tell him we were here. If she calls us and doesn't say anything to him about this fictitious check of great wealth, he's going to be pissed."

"We can protect her. I'm sure the two of us can stop him."

"You're about thirty pounds overweight and I'm getting too old to fight serial killers," he replied.

"That's what our guns are for, so I don't have to lose weight and you can grow old happily." We got to the car, entered, and sat. "Shall we wait here for him?"

"Do you know what he looks like?" Trapper asked.

"I saw a picture of him that Sue had on Greg's desk. He doesn't look so mean."

"He could be wiry. I hate wiry criminals, they don't fight nice," he moaned.

"You know you've gotten cranky as you get older."

"Better to be cranky than dead," he said.

"So shall we stake out here? See if he comes back soon."

Lonely Hearts Murders

"Let's give it an hour, then we'll decide if we'll stay longer,"

I agreed to that, and we sat watching the place. "Aren't you getting tired of playing detective?" Trapper asked me after a long pause.

I thought on that and said, "I do believe that I'm about ready to retire."

"You've retired more times than Cher on tour. If you're going to retire, you have to stay away from the office and actually do something else. You've got that motorhome, go travel."

"It's up to Penny. With her talk show, she can't just pack up and travel. She'd have to make a decision to retire also."

"I've heard Penny talking to Lacey about retiring. If you ask her, she may make up her mind to live with you in a mobile box. Traveling across the country like gypsies."

"My motorhome has all the conveniences of a home. I could very easily live in the thing."

"So, go. Every day I see you wandering the office looking for things to do and then don't do them. The only reason you're on this case is for your daughter, Carol."

"Now you're sounding like Lacey. Did she put you up to this?" I laughed.

"No, I guess we've been through a lot since we've been out here. How many times were you nearly killed? And Penny for that matter. You could have been a widower a number of times. Poor woman, kidnapped and tied up and taken across state lines. I'm surprised she hasn't divorced you."

"She loves me too much," I said, hoping she really did. I don't think I could find another woman like her. "Besides, I'd never let her divorce me."

"You do remember she is an expert marksman with a gun, right?" Trapper chuckled at that statement.

I didn't reply.

We sat for about forty minutes when a dark blue Audi pulled into the parking space out front of the apartment. A man stepped out of the car and stood looking around, then headed towards the apartment.

"Bingo, it's him."

"Shouldn't we call for back up?" Trapper asked.

I thought on that, and said, "I hate to say it, but you're right. No sense taking chances." I took out my cell phone then stopped. "But if I call Greg, he's going to bring in SWAT and ERT and then we'll have a real circus out here. All Conner would have to do is hold the woman hostage and then we'd have a standoff."

"Maybe we could get her out of there before the Calvary rushes in," Trapper offered.

I jumped when my cell phone buzzed. Caller ID said it was private. "This maybe her." I answered, "Hello?" and put it on speaker.

"Mr. Pierce? This is Kelly from Conner's apartment. He just got back," she said quietly.

"Where in the apartment are you?" I asked.

She hesitated, then said, "I'm in the bathroom." I could hear him yelling at the door for her to come out.

"Listen to me, go to the front door and run out now. We'll help you get away and stop him."

I heard the phone click off and looked at Trapper. "I hope she understood the urgency. Let's go to the door."

Lonely Hearts Murders

"Guns, unlocked and loaded," he said and we got out going back to the apartment. We could hear screaming from behind the door, then it flew opened and she came rushing out. We had our guns out and pointed at the opening of the doorway. Suddenly a man came around the corner yelling for her to get back in the apartment.

He froze when he saw us and our weapons. "What the hell?" he uttered.

Trapper yelled "Freeze, on the ground, face down, now!"

The man had his hand on the door and suddenly slammed it shut. Trapper took a couple shots at the door, I waited. "Damn," Trapper said. Suddenly gunshots rang out from behind the door and we scattered away.

"Okay, now he's mad," Trapper said as I pulled my cell phone out and speed dialed Greg. I looked back and saw the girl standing by the cars in the parking lot, looking terrified.

Greg answered and I said, "Got something for you if you can get here quickly. We've found Conner in an apartment and he's sort of holed up with a weapon. We'll watch him until you get here. Bring troops." I gave him the address and hung up.

"I called Greg. I hope he gets here fast," I told Trapper.

"Is there a back window he could climb out of?" Trapper asked. I went through the hallway leading to the back of the building and looked. There was one window and a door, they were still closed. I looked back to Trapper still standing away from the door, and said, "Nothing here."

A few minutes later I could hear sirens and four squad cars roared up. Greg and Sue jumped out of one car and came up to Trapper, still standing by the front of the building. I looked one more time to the window and then went to see them.

Trapper was explaining that we found Conner but he wasn't being very cooperative.

Lonely Hearts Murders

I was surprised that Greg didn't scold us for jumping his case. I was sure he was more than happy that Conner was found.

He told his men to watch the back and the side and said, "I have SWAT coming shortly, then they can enter the building."

I pointed to the woman and said it was her apartment that Conner had taken over. Sue went to the woman and brought her to us. Sue asked her name, she said Kelly.

"Kelly, is there any other way he could get out of the apartment?" Greg asked her.

"Just this door here and one in the back," she replied.

Greg had men on the back now and I didn't see him go out that way.

We suddenly heard gunfire coming from the back of the building and we all ran there except Sue and Kelly. I was concerned about what we would find.
        **

Chapter 14

Everyone stopped at the corner of the building and carefully looked around. We could see two officers on the ground and I saw a man running away. It was Conner. I pointed him out to Greg and he yelled for more men to follow Conner as he went to the downed officers. Luckily they were both still alive, just wounded. Greg called for an EMS and asked Trapper and me to guide the EMTs back here as he ran off in the direction Conner went.

I asked Trapper to wait with the wounded officers and went back to the front of the building. Sue and Kelly were still out front and I told them what happened. Sue ran to the back of the building, I presumed to follow the officers. Kelly stood looking lost.

"There are medical officers coming to take care of the wounded men. They can check you out also," I told her. I could hear a couple more gunshots in the distance. I hoped they nailed Conner. A couple minutes later an EMS unit roared up and parked. I took them to the wounded officers and brought Kelly with us.

They said the wounds were not bad, no damage to any vital areas. One officer was sitting up looking as if he were in shock. I wondered if he had ever been shot before. I doubted it by his expression. The Med Techs took them to the unit along with Kelly. They said they'd take her to the hospital for a checkup. Everyone piled into the unit and it drove off.

Trapper was standing next to me and said. "Well, it's up to Greg and his men to get Conner. What do you want to do now?"

"I need to know they have him in custody. I can't leave until we know that." We heard a couple more gunshots, further away now. I hoped they didn't get too far.

About ten minutes later, Greg came back with Sue. "We got him. He's wounded and will need medical treatment, but he's been arrested. Thanks for the heads up, guys," he said to Trapper and me.

I was glad he didn't get all police procedural on us for taking on Conner. "Is he being transported to the hospital?" I asked.

"Yeah, they have a unit over on the next street where the men are guarding him," Greg said. "I think they wanted to kick the crap out of him for shooting the other officers. I presume they're also on the way to the hospital?"

"They just rolled out about ten minutes ago and they took Kelly to be checked."

"Good, we can get her testimony about Conner being here," Greg said.

I looked at Sue and asked, "Are you going to take him back to Missouri?"

"I have to officially take custody, then I can turn him over to LVPD to file my paperwork that I had him in custody. Then

Lonely Hearts Murders

Nevada and Missouri can battle over who gets to prosecute him for the murders he did here and there."

Greg spoke, "As for the murder of Keller, we haven't any proof that Conner committed the crime. We can keep him for suspicion of murder, but if we don't have evidence, we can't hold him for long. Although, we have him for shooting two officers and fleeing the scene, that we can hold him for. I'm pressing charges on him for attempted murder."

"You'll have to work it out with Missouri because of the pending trial of the murders there," I said, then looked at Sue. "Did they have evidence that he committed the murders?"

"They had a strong case against him, but he fled before he could go to trial. It doesn't help his cause to have run," Sue said.

"Whatever," I said, "Greg, you'll have to work the evidence from Keller's murder now."

"Unfortunately, we don't have a lot to go on. I'm hoping CSI can find a link between Conner and Keller. With the fire that destroyed the escort service that you found, we don't have a connection there. Forensics has their computers and is going through them to see what they can find, but I was told not to hold my breath."

Two officers came around the back of the building and said that Conner was taken to the hospital. "Did anyone go with him?" Greg asked.

"Willis and Farnsworth rode in. They'll keep him guarded at the hospital," one officer said.

"Good, I'll file the paperwork for his arrest. Let's get out of here," Greg said and took Sue to his car. Everyone drove out except Trapper and me. We stood waiting for a moment.

"What's up?" Trapper asked.

Lonely Hearts Murders

"I'm just taking in all the recent events. Promotions, retirements, bounty hunter, new captain and catching a killer. Lots of fun stuff," I said.

"I think Conner was found too easily," he replied.

"Too easily? What do you mean?" I asked.

"We have a killer, then this woman rolls in and is looking for a killer, then it looks like he's our killer. She gives us a list of places he may be hiding and we find him, and catch him. All in a day's work. Too easy, and I don't believe in coincidences that Sue's killer is connected to the murder of Keller."

"Well, the M.O. is the same between the Missouri killer and ours. It seems like Conner is the likely suspect."

"Yes, and he was in all the cities when murders took place. But so were a lot of other killers."

"You don't think Conner killed Keller?" I asked.

"It's likely he did, but it's too convenient. I'm not saying that he didn't do it, but the guy comes into town and hires an escort, just to murder her. He has to be one sick puppy."

"No one said serial killers weren't sick, they are. I guess we need to look more into this to see if we can tie Conner in with Keller. Just to satisfy ourselves," I said.

"Where do we start?"

"We haven't talked to Carol yet. Maybe Keller shared more with her about her fatal date."

"Lead on, oh, great detective, I'll be right behind you if you fall," Trapper laughed and went to the car.

"Hey, you were supposed to follow," I yelled.

Lonely Hearts Murders

"Follow, lead, or get out of the way, that's my motto," he yelled back, laughing.

I really wondered about him most of the time. He was a goof-off, but I would have him on my side anytime. I went to the car and got in. We drove over to Mama Mia again and found Angelo talking to a waitress.

We waited until he was finished, then he came to us.

"Mr. R., I still haven't heard from my sources on the last two people on the list," he said.

"That's all right, we found the man, so tell your people thanks for helping. Now is Carol still in?" I asked.

"She's just finished up her shift. She should still be in the back. Why don't you go find a nice table and I'll send her to you."

We agreed and he went off. A few minutes later Angelo came out with Carol and they both sat at the table.

I started, "Carol, we need to talk."

**

Chapter 15

I could tell from the look in her eyes, she was worried. "It's not bad, Carol. We think we have a suspect in custody, but we still need to investigate."

"Who is the suspect?" she asked, looking relieved.

"I can't say, the investigation is still ongoing. He's in the hospital after being shot by police. They're guarding him, but I need to ask you a few questions, to clear things up."

"Ask me anything, I want to help," she said, sitting up now and looking harder.

"Good, now what was the last day you saw her?" I asked.

"Three days ago, when she last worked, before she vanished."

"Do you remember what you and she talked about?"

She paused, thinking. I gave her the time to gather her thoughts.

"She came into work and was excited. She found a company that would set her up with dates. Lisa was so upset that she had broken up with her boyfriend and wanted some companionship to take his place. So she said this company was just what she needed. I asked her where it was and she said it was over on Rancho Drive, a small building and there were about six people working there."

I looked at Trapper and said, "The building that was burned down wasn't on Rancho." I turned back to Carol and asked her to continue.

"She said she had a date that night, the one before she stopped coming into work. After we talked she went to work and that was the last I saw of her."

"Did she say what the name of the business was?"

"She did, but I can't remember the full name. It did have something about lonely hearts in it."

"Lonely Hearts Dating?" Trapper asked.

"I think that was it. Now that you mention, I think it was called Las Vegas Lonely Hearts Dating Service. Yes, I'm sure it was."

Now Trapper looked at me and said, "Definitely not the burned out escort service."

"Escort Service? Lisa did mention something about an escort service that she applied to work for. But she said she wasn't going to start with them right away. At least until after her dates with the Lonely Heart's people. She wanted to try that out first."

I sat back and took in this new information. Why was the escort service torched, if it had nothing to do with Keller's death? I know Trapper hated coincidences but this seemed to be one.

He was looking as perplexed as I felt. "Anything about the date she was supposed to have that last night you saw her?"

"She said she saw a photo of him and he was good looking. Blond wavy hair and a beard, like you wear, Dad. A Van Dyke, they call it."

I looked at Trapper and said, "If that was her last date, then it couldn't have been Conner. Besides, would a serial killer allow his face to be photographed?"

"Not a good idea," he replied. "Carol, you heard her tell you that was the man she was going out with that night she vanished," Trapper asked my daughter.

"That's what she said. As I think of it now, she did say his name, it was Jack Plunkitt. I thought it was an unusual name."

I turned to Trapper, "We need to go to Lonely Hearts and see about this Jack guy."

"I'm with you," he replied.

I stood and kissed my daughter on the forehead. "Listen to me carefully. If you meet a man, anywhere, you get his name and any information about him. Get it to me and I'll run a background check. I don't want you to take any chances. Understand?"

She gave me a big smile and agreed. I told her to go home and I'd call her later. She stood and left as I turned to Angelo, still sitting quietly and said, "If you can look up this Jack Plunkitt, see if he has a criminal past and contact me, I'd appreciate it." He stood and said he would.

Lonely Hearts Murders

We all left the room and Trapper lead me out to the car. "You're in an awful hurry aren't you? You keep getting ahead of me."

"Life is too short to slow down," he grinned and got in the car. "Do you know where this dating place is?"

"I have no idea," I said and took out my phone. I entered the name in the search box and it came up on Rancho Road. I had Trapper navigate and drove there.

"Should we call Greg with this new information?" Trapper asked. "After all, it is his case."

"He got his promotion, we can go on our own now," I said with a sly grin. "We can share after we find out what this is about."

"Fine with me. But he has a badge and they may give him information faster than we can get."

"If you do it just right we can bamboozle them into telling us what we want to know." I replied.

"Are you using the religious scam again?"

"No, that won't work. When we go in, I'll flash my auxiliary police badge that I got way back during the dirty bomb scare. If they don't look too closely, they'll assume we're cops."

"Religion and fake cops, you are getting devious," Trapper laughed.

"I watch a lot of TV."

We arrived at the dating service. It was a small building alone on the main road. The nearest business was a party store. We got out and went in. There was a girl at a counter and she smiled as we approached. I had my badge out before we got there and held it up.

"Hi, I was wondering if you could help us," I said as I put the badge back. Luckily, she didn't ask to see it closer. "We need some information about two of your clients, Lisa Keller and Jack Plunkitt."

"What is this in regards to?" she asked quickly.

"Well, Lisa Keller was murdered two nights ago, and she was supposed to be out on a date with Jack Plunkitt that night. We need information about Mr. Plunkitt so we can find him. All we need is an address."

"A client of ours was murdered by another?" she said looking shocked. "That's not good. If it will help you in your investigation, I'll see what we can do." She lifted her desk phone and made a call. About one minute later another woman came out through a door and to us.

"May I help you officers?"

"Investigators, ma'am. There was a murder two nights ago and it appears she was one of your clients and on a date with another. All we need is an address for the man she was out with that night so we can either clear him or arrest him."

"Two of our clients involved in murder? This could give us a black eye and frighten prospective clients away. Who was the man?"

"The name we have from a witness is Jack Plunkitt. Is he in your files?" I asked.

She turned to the computer on the desk and punched some keys. She studied the monitor and then said, "He is in our system."

**

Chapter 16

"Could we get his address?" I asked.

She stood and said, "Our client list is confidential, I'm sorry. You would need a warrant."

"Well, we can go get a warrant, but in the time it would take to get one, this man could murder another one of your female clients. I'm sure your company doesn't want that kind of publicity?"

She looked conflicted. "No, we don't. If you think you can stop this man from killing again, I'd say it was our civic duty to cooperate with you." She turned back to the computer and wrote on a pad of paper. She tore the top sheet off and handed it to me.

"Thank you. You may have saved a life." Trapper and I turned and went out of the building. We got back into the car and I looked at the address. "It's in North Vegas. I know the area," I started the car and drove over to the strip and went up.

"Do you think this Plunkitt guy could be our suspect?" Trapper asked as we went to the address.

"I haven't the faintest idea, until we talk to him," I replied.

"Are you going to call Greg?"

"I will, when we have something. Right now it's just what Carol heard from Keller. We don't know if she actually went out with Plunkitt."

We arrived at a house on Carey Avenue and parked. The house was one of a number of buildings that looked like they were run off on a photocopier. We found the right address and parked. There was no sign of life, the curtains were almost closed and no car in the drive.

"Well, let's see if someone is home," I said and we went to the front door. There was a doorbell and Trapper pushed it. We could hear a loud ring from in the house, but got no response.

"Maybe he's out," Trapper said and went to the front window. The curtain was mostly closed but there was a sliver of an opening. Trapper looked into the window then turned to me.

"Now would be a real good time to call Greg," he said.

"Why?" I asked.

"It looks like Jack Plunkitt is the late Jack Plunkitt."

I went to the window and looked in. Trapper was right. There was a body on the floor in a small pool of blood. "Well, that's not a good sign," I said as I pulled out my cell phone.

I dialed Greg and when he came on, I said, "Hey, Greg, got something new for you on the Keller murder." I told him we had a body and gave him the address.

About ten minutes later he showed up with Sue and one other squad car. The M.E. van came shortly after CSI showed. Trapper and I explained to Greg what we had found from talking to Carol.

"Maybe I should have started with Carol when this whole thing began," Greg said.

"We're working backwards ourselves. It may look like Conner didn't kill Keller, if she went out with Plunkitt the night she was murdered," I said.

We looked over as two officers were attempting to open the door to the house. They finally got it open and CSI went in first, along with the M.E. and his assistant. We stood waiting while they did their jobs.

A few minutes later the M.E. called to Greg and he went to the man standing at the door. They talked a minute and he handed Greg an evidence bag. Greg looked at it and came back to us.

"Jim, what was the name of the guy you were looking for?" he asked me.

"Jack Plunkitt," I replied.

"Well, the body in the house is not Plunkitt. It's some guy named Paul Lawrance. This is his address, so it must be his house."

"Well, then where is Plunkitt?" Trapper asked.

"Hiding? He may still be our killer then," Greg said.

As we stood there a car pulled up nearby and a woman got out. She rushed to us and said in a panic, "What's going on here? Where's my husband?"

Greg stepped up and asked, "You are?"

"Lynette Lawrance. My husband is Paul. Is he all right?" she said excitedly.

The M.E. rushed out to us and said, "I just called for a bus, the guy is still alive. I was sure he was dead, but he suddenly took a breath and opened his eyes. Scared the hell out of me. The blood loss was enough to kill, but he is alive, so far." He turned and went back in the house.

Now Mrs. Lawrance was losing it. "What is going on, please tell me!"

Sue pulled the wife aside and talked to her, hopefully explaining as gently as she could.

Greg, Trapper and I went to the door and looked in. Greg called to the supervisor of the CSI team and asked if we could enter.

"We're done now, you can come in," he replied.

Greg went to the M.E. who was working to keep the man alive. "I told the med techs that we would need plasma, since I don't know his blood type."

Lawrance was moaning softly. He opened his eyes and looked at Greg.

"Mr. Lawrance, who did this to you?" Greg asked.

Lawrance choked out "Jack…" then coughed hard.

"Let him rest, Greg. Ask your questions later."

Greg stood up and moved back to Trapper and me. "At least he managed to say Jack. I'll have a BOLO put out on him. If he didn't kill Keller, we can get him for this." Greg went out of the house followed by Trapper and me.

Sue was still with the wife, so Greg went to them. "Mrs. Lawrance, your husband is still alive. He was shot, but we need to know who the person was that did it. Do you know Jack Plunkitt?"

"Yes, he's a useless moocher. Paul let him stay with us, as much as I protested. I told Paul it would bite him on the ass if Plunkitt stayed here. Paul is a good person and hated to turn people away."

"How long has he been staying here?"

"About two weeks too long. Paul was finally going to tell him to leave. We had both had it with him."

An ambulance pulled up and the medics went to the house. A few minutes later they brought Lawrance out on a stretcher.

"You can go with him," Greg told the wife. She went to the van and they let her in. The doors closed and they drove off.

"So, Plunkitt is now high on my suspect list," Greg said and turned to Sue. "Other than shooting the officers, it looks like Connor is off the hook for the murder of Keller. I suppose your murder is more important than his wounding of our police. I think Missouri can take him, but it's up to the D.A. to decide."

"Either way, as long as he's in custody, I'm good," Sue said.

The CSI team came out of the house. "We got a number of prints if they will help in finding your man," the supervisor said to Greg.

"Thanks, Mike. Send me the results," Greg replied.

My cell phone buzzed and I saw it was Angelo. "Hey, Angelo, what's up?"

"I checked around and found out that your man has a reputation for being a killer-for-hire. He's a hitman."

**

Chapter 17

That sort of surprised me, but I half expected it. "Thanks for that Angelo, I'll pass it along to Greg Warren." We finished and hung up.

I went to Greg and told him what Angelo said. "Well, that puts a different perspective on this. Now I have to get a warrant for his arrest," Greg said and went aside to use his cell phone.

Trapper came over to me and said, "I guess Plunkitt isn't coming back here any time soon."

"I think he would be better off not coming back," I said sarcastically. "Now we have to find him, wherever he could be."

"Why did Plunkitt give his information to the dating service? He listed this as an address, didn't he think the police would figure it out and come here?" Trapper said.

"I'm thinking he's either new to the hitman business, or he's really arrogant."

"Or stupid," Trapper added.

"True. But he's probably moved on. I doubt he'll go back to Lonely Hearts, but it wouldn't hurt to alert them in case he does. As you said, he may be stupid and want another date."

"Riddle me this, Batman," Trapper said with a grin. "Why would a hitman sign up with a dating service? Is he a lonely serial killer for hire or just a whack-job, getting his kicks murdering lonely women?"

"Batman?" I replied. "Your guess is as good as mine, Joker. This is getting confusing, what with Conner following the M.O., but now it looks like Plunkitt was the killer. So where does that leave Conner? Did Plunkitt copycat Conner or are they working together?"

"I'm ready to go back to the office and find a nice spousal cheating case. Are we done here?" Trapper asked.

I looked around and saw we were by ourselves. Everyone else was going to their cars and leaving, except CSI. They were still gathering the equipment in their van. I signaled to Trapper to follow and went to my car.

We drove back to the office in silence. I was going over the events of the last couple days, trying to piece it together. We arrived and went in the building, going up to the front. I was surprised to see Lorelei Paris talking to Penny and Lacey. The women turned to us and laughed.

"Now what did I do that was so funny?" I asked.

"We were just talking about you, that's all, and you showed up," Penny said.

Lonely Hearts Murders

I went to Lorelei and said, "Congratulations on your promotion and taking over for Weber." I held out my hand and she shook it. "Now, why are you here?"

"I wanted to get your side of this murder of Lisa Keller. I know Greg is doing his best, but I wanted an outside opinion of the case, before I take over the precinct. You always seem to have good opinions on murders."

"Well, we're stymied on this one. We have two killers and we're not sure which one murdered Keller. Why don't you come into my office and we'll talk." I smiled at Penny and turned to go back to my office. I figured Trapper would follow, he liked to look at Lorelei. Penny would follow to make sure I didn't look at her too much.

We all filed into my office and I picked up Willy, sleeping on my chair and handed him to Penny. I asked everyone to sit and then said, "I'll give you the rundown of what happened from when my daughter came to ask me to find a missing friend of hers from work.

I spent the next half hour going over details of what Trapper and I found as Trapper also offered his side of the story.

"Well," Lorelei said after I finished. "This is going to be a he-said, he-said, type of case. We have Conner under guard at the hospital and I'm sure Greg will track down Plunkitt. Then we need to sort out this mess. What's your opinion?"

I thought about it and said, "I'm honestly not sure. Conner murdered a woman in Missouri the same way Keller was murdered and one other woman a year ago here in Vegas. It fits the pattern for him. But from what we were told, Keller was out on a date with Plunkitt the night she was murdered. He seems the likely suspect."

"But why would he murder a woman that others knew he was on a date with," Penny asked. "Seems stupid to me. Why not just grab a woman and kill her? Why leave a trail?"

"My thoughts, also. We won't know until Plunkitt is in custody and questioned," I responded to her questions.

"Well, thanks for filling me in. I'm taking command of the precinct this weekend and I wanted to be up on this case. I'll be talking to Greg to pick his brain also. I'm not mentioning that I talked to you first, I don't want Greg to feel slighted."

"Good idea. Greg has worked hard to get where he is now. I'm sure he'll figure this out," I said.

"I have to go get my things ready to put in Weber's office. He's already talked to me this morning about the men and what they are like. But then, I have worked in the precinct twice before, so I sort of know what to expect."

"I'm glad you're taking over. Weber was a good Captain, but he was a little standoffish when it came to solving crime. As long as you come in with the right attitude, you'll do fine," I said.

"Thanks, Jim. Good to see all of you and I hope we'll be working together again," she paused then said, "Penny, would you like to go grab a bite to eat? I'd like to talk to you about fashions, ones that state that I'm in charge."

"I'd be happy to. Shall we go to Mama Mia's?"

"Sounds good to me," Lorelei said and stood. "Thanks, Jim and Will, I like to be prepared and you helped." Lorelei and Penny went out of the room, after Penny handed Willy to me.

"She's still a good looking woman," Trapper said after the women left.

"She is," I said. "I'm sure that won't distract the detectives from following her orders. When I worked with her, she was tough in the field and in the office," I said.

Trapper stood and said, "I'll talk to you later. I need to catch up on other things." He left the office, leaving me alone with Willy. The dog was sitting on my desk looking at me with a cute expression, I had to laugh.

I stood and picked up the dog, leaving my office heading toward the back door. I found Fred in his room and asked, "Is Henry in the dog run?"

"He is. I just put him out there to get some fresh air," he replied. "Do you want me to put Willy out there?"

"Sure, that would be nice. Thanks," I said and handed the dog to Fred.

"I'll leave them out there for an hour or so and then bring them in," Fred said as he went to the back door and out.

I stood in the hallway wondering what to do, when my cell phone buzzed. I pulled it out and looked at the caller ID, it was Angelo. Now what did he find, I wondered.

**

Chapter 18

I answered. "Hey, Angelo, is this a social call?" I asked.

"Mr. R. I got some more info on your suspects," he said in my ear. I hoped it was good news. "It seems Plunkitt spent some time in High Desert State Prison here in Clark County, back a year ago, then he was released. Your man Conner was also in that prison at the same time. I don't believe in coincidences, but that seems to be one."

I thought on that. "Well, it could be that they knew each other then. That would explain why the killings were so similar. Do you know what they were in for?"

"Plunkitt was in for beating a woman nearly to death. There was overcrowding in the prison, so he was let out early. Conner was in for assaulting a woman prostitute, he was stopped by an undercover cop before he could do any real harm. He was let out for the same reason, overcrowding."

"So they both have violent tendencies towards women. It helps, thanks. Do me a favor and thank your network of friends, they're a big help." I said. He said he would tell them and hung up. I knew it would be a matter of time for Greg to find this information. I hoped. I had my own way of finding out who's bad or good and I don't have to bother the police. It's just strange to depend on mob wiseguys to get that information.

I sat for a few minutes, then Trapper came rushing in. "Jim, I just got a call from a friend on the force who knew I was involved with capturing Conner. He said Conner escaped from the hospital about 30 minutes ago. He took a nurse hostage and went to a car waiting in the parking lot. He had an accomplice. He also took the nurse with him."

"Why didn't the police watching him just shoot him?" I asked.

"He had a gun, they don't know how he got it, but he was threatening to kill the nurse."

"I wonder if Plunkitt helped him and slipped him the gun," I said. "I just talked to Angelo and he found out that Conner and Plunkitt were in prison together. Plunkitt has to be the accomplice. I hope I'm wrong, but I'm sure they'll find the nurse dead."

"So maybe Conner and Plunkitt worked the killings together? But what about Missouri? Was Plunkitt there too?" Trapper asked.

"Good question. Maybe Plunkitt only works out of Vegas and Conner ended up in Missouri after he was released from prison, but came back here to see Plunkitt," I said.

"Anything is possible at this time. Do you think Angelo and his network could track them down?" Trapper asked.

Lonely Hearts Murders

"It's a good thought. Hold on," I said and lifted my desk phone. I called Angelo back and he came on. "Angelo, it's Jim. I have another big favor to ask. George Conner escaped police custody and it looks like Plunkitt may have helped him. Do you think your people could track them down?" I put the phone on speaker so Trapper could hear.

"For you, sure. I'll get right on it," Angelo said.

"One other thing, they took a nurse hostage from the hospital. I'm sure her life is in danger with the men. Time is important."

"I get ya, Mr. R. and I'll make it a priority to find them," he said and hung up.

"Well, the mob is now involved in the hunt. Think I should warn Greg?" I asked.

"Wait until you have something to go on. No sense getting Greg all stirred up."

Penny came back in the room, surprising me. "That was a quick lunch," I said.

"Lorelei got a call about a manhunt for the killer of Carol's friend. Seems he escaped from the hospital, and they want everyone back to the precinct to help find him," Penny explained. "So Lorelei is having to start her command early."

I looked at Trapper and said, "Maybe I should call Lorelei and let her know about the connection between Conner and Plunkitt."

"It may help her. But I think you should let Greg in on it first, then let him tell Lorelei." Trapper said.

"Yeah, that's a good idea. I'm not telling Greg who my sources are, just give him the info and he can look it up himself."

Penny sat in my client chair and said, "I have no idea what you two are talking about, but I'm sure it's good."

"It is, now I have to get hold of Greg," I said and pulled over my desk phone, calling him. He came on and I put the phone on speaker. "Greg, Jim here. I have some information that may help you with Conner and Plunkitt."

"Talk to me, I need anything right now that will help," he replied.

I told him everything that I found out about Conner and Plunkitt being in prison together. I didn't tell him who told me, I just said it came from my sources.

"That wouldn't be from your underworld sources," Greg said with a laugh.

"I plead the fifth. Now see what you can do with that info. It should be just a matter of time to connect the two of them to find out where they may be."

He thanked me and hung up. "I hope he puts it to good use." I said. "I'm going to the break room and get a sandwich from the new machine."

"Enjoy your lunch, I've got some errands to run. I'll be back," Trapper said and left the room. I stood and took Penny to the break room and bought us lunch.

"Big spender on our lunch. Tuna on rye, I guess I'll survive," Penny said as I handed her the sandwich. She tore open the package and ate the thing.

"I was talking to Trapper the other day about retiring. What do you think about that?" I asked her.

"I thought you already retired? You haven't done much other than take this case and you did that because of Carol," she replied with a grin.

"I sort of did, but I need something to get me away from the office. I mentioned to Will that I might enjoy traveling in the motorhome." I waited for her to respond.

She sat munching on her sandwich and looking like she was thinking. "If you did that you'd have to take me, right?"

"I wouldn't go without you," I replied.

"So, that would mean that I would have to retire also. I think Gordy would have a heart attack, but he could always find someone to take my place. There are enough celebrities living in Vegas to do it."

"So, do you think it would be on the bucket list?" I said. "We would travel the country, this time without doing book signings."

"Yes, speaking of your books, are you going to do another one?"

"No, I decided that I'm retiring from that also. I've gotten worn out from writing and my book sales have been declining. So why write more if no one is buying?"

"Good point. So you're starting a new direction with your life. No playing detective and no playing author, correct?"

I smiled and said, "That's the plan."

**

Chapter 19

"I'll have to think about it. Give me a day or two. I've been doing my talk show for almost seven years, even before I met you. It will be hard to retire, but I may be ready to do this."

I smiled and said, "Take your time, you have to be ready to make the move. I've been slowly doing this for a while so it's easy for me. I started this firm from a one room office in Michigan and built it up to this," I said waving my hand around the room. "It's been a great journey and many friends along the way."

"True, give me a few days, then I'll decide," Penny said.

Lacey came to the door and said, "Jim, you have a visitor."

"Who?" I asked.

Lonely Hearts Murders

"Sue Hanson, bounty hunter," she said with a smirk.

"Would you bring her to my office?" I asked. We stood and went to my office and sat waiting.

Lacey came in a short time later with Sue Hanson. I stood and said, "Welcome, come in and sit," I said directing her to a chair next to Penny. "Now, what brings you back here?" I asked sitting at my desk.

"I'm going to be honest, I came here looking for my bounty. He was in custody, now he's not. I'm not happy about this. I like Greg, although we haven't seen each other in years, he's different. Maybe it's me, I don't know, but I need to find Conner and get him back to Missouri. Since it looks like he didn't murder your girl, I shouldn't have to worry about jurisdiction."

"So, what do you want me to do?"

"I know that you are feeding Greg information about Conner and Plunkitt, so you must have a better source for finding my man. I'll split the bounty on Conner if you'll help me capture him."

"I don't want to alienate Greg, he's a friend and my only source in the police since I've hired all the previous sources away from LVPD. I may be able to help you, but I don't really need to split the bounty with you. If we can do this without alerting the police, I'm game."

"Good, do you have any idea where Conner may have gone?"

"Well, the police have put out a dragnet for him, so he may have to stay in Vegas a little longer. My sources are looking for him and they have a bit more influence than the police."

"I heard Greg talking to the new lady Captain, he said you have underworld connections with a mob figure."

Lonely Hearts Murders

I laughed at her reference to Angelo being a mob figure. "He has connections, but he gave up the life long ago. His connections still respect him and give him help when he asks. I'm just waiting for word from him. So we just have to wait. Do you have a place to stay?"

"Greg has been so busy that he hasn't set me up yet. I'll just go find a motel and settle."

Penny spoke up, "No, we have a guesthouse that you can use until you catch your man."

I was surprised that she offered the guesthouse. "Sure, it's vacant right now and if you enjoy swimming, Penny would love the company." Penny beamed when I said that.

"Well, that's really nice of you, thank you," she said happily.

Penny stood and asked, "Do you have luggage?"

"In my rental car I do."

"Okay, you can follow me to the house. Jim can call if anything breaks in finding your man." She looked at me and I gave her a thumb up. "Good, shall we go?"

Sue stood and they both went out of the office leaving me alone, again. I looked at Willy still on my desk, "Shall I move to the couch?" Willy was bouncing now.

I was getting ready to rest on the couch. I had my door closed and a note on the door to not disturb me. Before I could plop down, my cell phone buzzed. Caller ID said it was Angelo.

"Damn, I can never rest," I said as I answered. "Angelo, did you find out something?"

"Sorry, Mr. R. but Conner has gone deep. Plunkitt was spotted about an hour ago, in McCarran Airport. The police spotted him and he ran, right into my people. We have him in a warehouse by the airport."

Lonely Hearts Murders

"Have they talked to him?"

"I told them to wait for you."

"Thank you, my friend, give me the address." He read off the address and I wrote it down. I told him I was on my way, and we finished the call. I thought about calling Greg, but I wanted to find Conner first. I called Penny and asked to talk to Sue. She came on and I told her that Plunkitt was being held captive. I said I'd come get her and we could go talk to him.

Twenty minutes later, I had Sue and Penny in my car. Penny insisted on joining us. I drove out by the airport and found the building. There were two burly men standing by the side door who gave us a wary eye as we approached.

"I'm Jim Richards, Angelo said to come here."

They both smiled and one opened the door for us. We went in and found four more men standing around Plunkitt, who was tied to a chair in the middle of a large open area.

Angelo turned to me and grinned. "Mr. R., we waited for you. He's been real quiet."

I grabbed a chair from nearby and told everyone else to find one and sit. Angelo pulled two chairs for Sue and Penny. I sat in front of Plunkitt. He had minor bruises on his face, I presumed fighting to get away from Angelo's men.

"Jack, I'm sorry we had to meet like this. My problem is not with you, I just want to know where Conner is. Simple, you tell me and we won't hurt you."

I looked at a big bruiser standing behind Plunkitt. I winked at him and he smacked Plunkitt in the back of the head. Not a hard tap but enough to shake Plunkitt up a little.

"That was just a love tap, Jack. Do you know who these men are? No? Well, they all are members of organized crime families. You are just a murderer but these men make crime their living. I'm sure if you added up all the people who ended up in shallow desert graves or at the bottom of Lake Mead, it would stagger you. You don't want to end up like that, do you, Jack?"

He was looking around at the men moving closer now. He started to sweat and his eyes went bigger.

"Again, just tell me where Conner is and I'll see you just get a nice cushy jail cell and a court trial. Maybe you'll even get off," I paused, "So, where's Conner?"

He held his tongue, not speaking. I stood and moved away. "I don't condone violence, but you are a killer." I looked to Angelo, "Think your men can make him talk?"

Angelo grinned, "Just like the old days," he said with a smile.

**

Chapter 20

"Let me take the ladies out first," I said and told Penny and Sue to follow. They both protested but I told them I wanted them to have deniability as to what was going to happen. They stood and followed me out.

We stood by the cars, barely hearing screams from the building. "I don't like this," Penny said.

"Neither do I, but think about the women this animal killed in cold blood. Including Carol's friend. How many times when you were kidnapped did you bash the heads of your captors with pipes and a fire extinguisher? I'm sure you felt that was justified. Not to mention the couple bad men you shot dead."

She didn't reply.

Lonely Hearts Murders

"If we can get two animals off the streets, it has to be done," I said just as the door opened and Angelo came out.

"He wasn't much of a fight. He talked real fast when Marco suggested that we…" he paused looking at the women. "Well, there was a suggestion made and Plunkitt decided to spill the beans."

Angelo handed me a piece of paper. "This is where you'll find Conner. If he hasn't moved."

"Thanks my friend. Now have everyone scatter, leaving Plunkitt alone in the building. I'm calling Greg Warren and giving him Plunkitt's location."

"Will do Mr. R., do you want I should send some men with you to nab Conner?"

"Let me look over the situation and if I need backup, I'll call."

Angelo went to the door and yelled in, "Okay, everyone split, make haste, cops are coming." A few seconds later, there was a flurry of feet as Angelo's associates rushed out and left. Angelo looked in one more time then gave me a thumb up, smiled and went to his car.

The three of us got in my car and sat as I pulled my cell phone and dialed Greg. I listened while it rang, then Greg answered. "Hello?"

"Greg, this is Jim, how would you like to take Plunkitt into custody?"

"It's one of my goals right now, why?"

"I can tell you where he is, but you'll have to make a promise."

"I'm listening," he said.

"If anyone asks you how you found him, you will say it was an anonymous tip. Can you do that?"

"If I can arrest Plunkitt, I guess I could tell a little lie, but why the secrecy?"

Lonely Hearts Murders

"Well, Plunkitt isn't in great shape and you don't need any more info than that. If asked, I'll deny I knew anything about him. Got it?"

There was a pause, "I don't suppose your little friends had anything to do with this?"

"Again, need to know. And you don't need to know."

"What about Conner?" Greg asked.

"I'm working on that, I'll let you know." I gave him the address and hung up.

"Now we go find Conner," I said and started the car, driving out of the parking lot.

"Penny, call Trapper and ask him to find Earl and have both of them come to this address," I said, handing her the paper with the address. She pulled out her cell phone and dialed Trapper, explaining my request. She hung up and said, "He's on his way after he finds Earl."

"Good, I don't want the mob getting involved in this," I said.

"You had them involved with Plunkitt?" Penny asked me.

"They had already caught him. I want Sue and us to take down Conner. Now where are we going?"

"You don't know?" Penny asked.

"I know the road, but not which way to go when we get there."

Penny made a tsking noise with her tongue and took out her phone again and looked up the address on Google. She found the address and navigated.

We got to the street and I stopped a short distance from the address we were given. It was a house, standing alone on a large lot. The neighboring houses were far apart, which I presumed was good for Conner.

"Well, are you going to attack?" Penny asked with a grin.

"Not by myself, I'm not stupid. We'll wait until Trapper and Earl get here," I said as I saw a car pulling up behind me. It was Trapper's Jeep and I could see him, and Buck was in the passenger seat.

They got out and came to my car squeezing in the back seat with Sue.

"I presume you couldn't find Earl?" I asked.

"Nope, Buck was handy, and he's more dangerous than Earl," Trapper said.

"Thank you, Will," Buck said, "even if you don't believe it," he laughed to himself.

"Whatever, I was told by Angelo from the information Plunkitt gave out that Conner is supposed to be here. Do you two have your guns?"

They both agreed and I said, "Okay, let's go see what we have." I opened my door after telling Penny and Sue to stay.

"I have my gun too," Penny said.

"I'm happy for you, but I don't want to lose you now. So stay," I demanded. She agreed.

I got out of the car as Trapper and Buck came around to me. "Let's not get him riled enough to start shooting. If we can surprise him, it will be better for all."

We went down the street to the house, but stopped at a stand of bushes and short trees next to the house. We watched the place and saw no movement, so we went up to the building, keeping close to the outside walls. I went to a window and peeked in. I saw nothing.

We went around to the back and looked in the window and still saw nothing. "Maybe he isn't here," Trapper said.

Lonely Hearts Murders

"He could be out grabbing a new victim," Buck said.

I looked at him and said, "Don't even think that. Maybe he's just out for a burger. Let's see if we can get in the house."

Trapper went up to the back door and tried it. The thing wasn't locked. "Not a smart thing to do. You never can tell if a burglar will come in."

"I'm sure Conner isn't worried about burglars," I said. "Move in carefully."

We went in and cleared the house, Conner was not there. "Well, this sucks, I hoped we'd find him sleeping," I said.

"Well, he's not here, shall we go back to the cars and wait?" Trapper said.

"That's about all we can do," I said as Buck came out of the hallway from the bedrooms.

"You're not going to like this," he said solemnly. We followed him back to a door and went in. On the bed was the body of a woman, bleeding out from a wound in the back of her head, It was the nurse, judging by her clothes.

"Damn, too late to help her. Let's get out of here and go to the cars. I'll call Greg and get him involved." We went out of the bedroom and through the kitchen. It was a mess, littered with beer cans and food wrappers. Even I wouldn't live like this alone. I led the way out the back door after checking to see if Conner was hiding in the backyard. There was a small garage that I would have liked to check out, but we needed to get away from the house.

We went back to the cars and I saw that Penny and Sue were not in my car. I stood looking around but didn't see them. "What the hell," I uttered.

My cell phone buzzed and I saw it said Penny on the caller ID. "Where are you?" I asked when I answered.

I heard a man's voice.

**

Chapter 21

"Not a smart move to leave the women alone," the voice said, as I put it on speaker for Trapper and Buck to hear.

"Conner, you are a dead man. I was going to turn you over to the police, but you just had to go too far. Your life is mine," I threatened.

"Now, I suggest you and your friends get in your cars and drive away."

"Not on your life," I spouted.

"No, but on the life of your women you will. Now go." He hung up.

I clicked off the phone and said, "He has to be nearby to see if we leave." I stood looking around at the houses and woods in the area. "I have faith that Penny can get out of this situation as she has in the past. Plus with Sue, the two of them should be able to handle Conner," I said, hoping I was right.

"Jim, this guy is an experienced killer," Trapper said. "Those other guys that Penny took on were just wimps compared to Conner."

I knew he was right, which worried me even more. "We need to interrogate Plunkitt to find out if they have another place to hide out. Let's leave so he won't hurt them for now," I said, taking one last look around the area. I held my middle finger high in the air so he could see it and got in the car. Trapper went to his car with Buck and followed me out.

I drove over two streets and pulled in. I figured the terrain was busy enough so he couldn't see us. I parked and got out. Trapper and Buck came to me and waited. I pulled out my cell phone and dialed Greg, putting the phone on speaker so Trapper and Buck could hear. He came on and I asked, "Are you with Plunkitt?"

"We just got here a short time ago. What did your men do to him?"

"First off, they aren't my men. They don't do what I say, they just don't like killers like Plunkitt and Conner. Now shut up and listen. Conner has Penny and Sue."

"What!" Greg exploded through the phone. "How did that happen?"

"Long story. If you still have Plunkitt tied to the chair, I would suggest you send everyone out and do your best to question him as to where Conner could have another hideout other than the one he gave me."

There was a long pause. I wondered if Greg was going to be a boy scout about this. I hoped he would react like a wiseguy and beat the info out of Plunkitt.

I heard him say, "I'll call you back." He hung up and I hoped he would do the right thing.

I stood by the car feeling helpless. This wasn't the first time Penny was taken hostage, but not by a serial killer. Trapper and Buck stood by me, as Buck yelled, "Look!" He was pointing to the main road off the street we were on. It was Sue running across the end of our street.

I yelled, "Sue," as loudly as I could, joined by Trapper and Buck. She disappeared past our street then a few seconds later she came back cautiously looking towards us. We were waving to her and she ran to us.

"Where's Penny?" I asked as she came running up.

"Penny started to get rough with Conner, beating on him, long enough for me to get away. I didn't want to leave her, but I didn't have my gun, Conner took it."

"Where are they?" I asked.

"In a van on the street," she said.

I thought back and remembered the van. "Damn, it was right by us."

"He's probably gone by now," Trapper said.

I looked at Trapper and said, "Take a ride by the street and see if he's still there. Call me if he is." Trapper and Buck went to the Jeep and drove out. I turned to Sue and told her to get in the car and rest. She climbed in the back seat and sat looking out.

I saw Trapper's Jeep coming back to the street and that worried me. He parked and came to me. "The van is gone, sorry, Jim."

"Okay, we have a crime scene with the dead nurse. I'll call Greg again and see what he's got." I pulled my cell phone and dialed him.

He came on and said, "I'll call you back, Jim." Then he hung up.

I stood looking at my phone wondering if he was busy interrogating Plunkitt. I was feeling a knot in my stomach not knowing where Penny was. I knew she was tough, but could she handle Conner?

I speed dialed Lorelei and told her where the house with the nurse was.

"Where's Greg?" she asked.

"Uh, he's interrogating Jack Plunkitt. I called him about the nurse and he said he was with Plunkitt. It's a complicated story, but just go with it, I'll explain later."

"I'll send a team to the house, but you need to bring me up to speed," she said.

"I'll say the house was where Conner was hiding, so tell forensics to keep that in mind," I said.

"I'll take care of it, thanks," she said and hung up.

"Well, the nurse's body will be taken care of. Now we need to find Conner and Penny. I hope he starts something with me so I can shoot him. But you didn't hear that."

"Hear what," Buck said. "You talk so much I rarely listen." He laughed, then stopped. "Sorry, Jim. We'll find Penny."

"I'm sure we will. I'm hoping she works him over." I frowned and turned to the car and Sue. I leaned in and said, "Did you hear anything Conner said while you were being held?"

Sue thought a moment and said, "Penny and I were talking in the car when Conner opened Penny's door and pulled her out. I would have pulled my gun but he held Penny up with his gun at her head, and I wouldn't have a clean shot. He ordered me out of the car and to a van nearby. He put us in the back and asked Penny for her phone. She gave it to him after he threatened to shoot me. He went through her contacts and asked who the man was at the house. Penny told him. He called and you know the rest after that." She paused.

I waited for her to finish, I could tell she was upset. "How did you get away?"

"After Conner watched you drive away he relaxed a little. Penny brought her leg up and hit him in the stomach. Then they fought, which left me an opening to get out of the van through the back doors. I ran, and as much as I hate myself for not helping Penny, I was afraid for my life." She looked totally upset and didn't say more.

"Sue, it's something you had to do. I'm sure Penny understands and is glad you got away. I'm sure Conner will keep Penny alive, he needs her as a hostage. If she dies, his life is forfeit."

**

Chapter 22

I had no idea what to do next. I had to depend on Greg Warren to get Plunkitt to talk. I hoped Penny was all right and I could get my hands on Conner.

"Let's go back to the place where Plunkitt is being held," I said. We all got in our cars and drove out. On the main road I could see patrol cars pulling onto the street where the nurse was. I drove back to the building and pulled in just as Greg was coming out of the building. There were four other officers standing outside of the building.

I parked and went to Greg. "Did you get anything from him?" I asked.

"No specific address, but he said Conner liked to hang out at a bar on Chene. Maybe someone there would know where Conner could be. I'm going there now," he said, then instructed two uniforms to take Plunkitt in custody. He was heading for his car and stopped upon seeing Sue coming towards us.

"Sue! I thought Conner had you?" Greg said excitedly.

"He did, but I got away. Now we have to save Penny," Sue replied.

"Come with me," Greg said to her and led her to his car. I followed them out, with Trapper and Buck behind me. The two patrol cars were right behind us with flashers and sirens going. Greg sped to the bar and when we found it, parked.

All of us went into the bar and spread out at the door. It was fairly quiet, a slow song on the juke box, which was unplugged by one of the officers on Greg's command. The people in the bar made rude comments.

"Shut up, everyone," Greg said holding up his badge. Two of the four officers moved up next to him. The other two guarded the door. "I'm looking for a wanted man, George Conner. If you know where he could be, talk now, or I'll have everyone here taken in for questioning. I don't think some of you would want to be in a police station, so talk."

They all grew quiet, not a word. "I'm giving you a pass on any charges if you help me. Again, talk."

One man, a biker type, stood from his stool at the bar and went to Greg. The cops were ready in case he pulled anything. Greg stood his ground.

"What's he wanted for?" the biker growled.

"Murder and kidnapping, do you know him?" Greg asked boldly.

The big man paused, looked around and said quietly, "What's in it for me?"

"You got any warrants?"

He thought and said, "Yeah, one. For a bar fight."

"I'll make it go away. Talk to me."

"He hangs at two places when he's in town," the man said. I was next to Greg when he gave the street name of the house where the nurse was found.

"We've been there," I said. Greg looked at me and I told him I would explain later. "What is the other place?" I asked the biker.

"Don't know the address, but I can take you there," he said.

"So, let's move it. We have to rescue a woman. Maybe I'll get you a citation."

The biker grinned and said, "Well, move it."

He headed to the door and the two officers moved aside. We all went out to the parking lot as the man got on his motorcycle and started it up. "Don't get too far ahead of us," Greg yelled over the noise.

Once again we all drove out following the biker as he led us to an area of buildings and factories that looked run down and boarded up.

We parked on the street as the biker got off his cycle. He pointed to the building in front of us. "He hides out here, when he's running. It's all deserted in this area. Now are you going to delete my warrant?" he asked Greg.

Greg pointed to one of the officers and said to get his information. Then he said to the man, "It will be done, if Conner is here. Now stay around until we have Conner in custody."

"Hell, man, he'll die first before you'll take him down."

"That's fine with me, saves us a lot of problems." Greg called for back-up and told the four men to spread out around the building. I could see a van on the side of the building and told Greg it may be Conner's.

About ten minutes later a SWAT team pulled up and the van opened pouring out about six men in protective outfits. The captain of the team came to Greg and said they were ready.

"Okay, but we have to be careful. This man has a hostage, Penny Wickens, so we have to be on alert for her."

The captain explained to his men the plan to go in. Everyone ran carefully to the building, keeping low. Greg and the captain went to a window that wasn't boarded up completely. They discussed their options as I tried to listen in, but they were being too quiet.

Trapper, Buck and I went around the building to search on our own. The police were organized but I worried about Penny. We found a door on the side and I tried it. It wasn't locked, so the three of us went in.

Lonely Hearts Murders

"Let's not get shot by friendly fire," I said, as we crept around a lot of rusty machinery.

I could hear music ahead, and slowly went to it. We hid behind a large piece of machinery as I peeked around it. There was a small area set up like a place to crash. A couch, chairs, tables and a bed were on an old carpet in the middle of the room. Conner was relaxing in one easy chair listening to music coming from what looked like a boom box. I looked for Penny, but didn't see her.

"She must be nearby, I hope," I said quietly to Trapper, right behind me.

I could see a window where there was movement. It had to be Greg or the SWAT leader. Either way, they had a handle on the situation.

"We need to find Penny," I said and went around the machinery to the other side of the room. Conner must have been asleep, for he didn't move each time I looked out to him. I saw a door on the side of the room, probably a former office. I pointed it out to Trapper and Buck and we moved around the room to the door. I stopped and realized that it was in direct sight of Conner. If we went to the door he would see us.

I looked around and saw that he had his head back and his eyes closed. "I'm going to the door, stay here and watch Conner." I moved quietly to the door and tried the knob. It was locked. Now I didn't know what to do. Break in and wake Conner or wait until Greg and SWAT came in with guns blasting.

"Penny?" I whispered at the door. I heard a noise and a muffled voice. It was her, I knew that little cry for help.

I brought my foot up, hit the door knob and it burst open. The noise was loud enough to wake the dead and Conner. He jumped up with his gun out, blasting at the office. I tackled Penny tied to a chair and hoped we didn't get hit. I suddenly heard more gunfire, I presumed Trapper and Buck were joining in on the shooting.

I covered my wife as I heard doors crashing and loud voices now from Greg and the team. There was more blasting, then it was silent.

**

Chapter 23

I took out my pocket knife and cut Penny loose. I carefully pulled the tape from her mouth.

"About time you got here," she said. I put the tape back over her mouth and stood, going to the door, looking out. Trapper and Buck were by the door and I could see the SWAT team all standing around a body on the floor. I presumed it was Conner, but couldn't see him with all the legs between me and the body.

"We, or they, got him. He was shooting at your direction when Buck and I started shooting back. Then Greg and the SWAT guys came busting in and started firing. I'm sure Conner is full of holes," Trapper said with a grin.

Penny and I came out of the room, as Sue came over to Penny and they hugged. Sue turned to me and said, "I'm glad you found her safely."

"So am I," I replied.

Penny and Sue went over to Greg and the body. I stayed by Trapper and Buck.

"Well, this case is closed," Buck said.

"I hope so. We still don't really know if Conner murdered Keller, but it's irrelevant now, I suppose," I said. "We have Plunkitt, who was supposed to be on a date with her. Maybe he did it, or not. I'm sure Greg will find out after interrogating Plunkitt."

Lonely Hearts Murders

"Let's get out of here," Penny said, coming back to me. I agreed.

Trapper and Buck said they were going back to the office. I said I'd take Penny home, it was getting late.

We all left the building. It was starting to get dark now and the coroner had just arrived. I drove back home and parked in the garage. Penny went in the house and by the time I reached the bedroom, she was undressed and under the covers.

"How do you do that?" I asked.

"I love being in bed, so I move quickly. What's taking you so long?" she said with a sly grin.

I was in bed in record time.

"Have you given thought about retiring now after what happened today?" I asked.

"It's on my mind. My show doesn't get me kidnapped. You need to retire to get away from criminals," she laughed quietly under the covers.

"Okay, I'm retired. Officially. So when do you tell Gordy that you're moving on?"

"I'll think about it," she replied.

"That's your problem, you think too much." I snuggled up to her and kissed her ear. "Feel like fooling around?"

"I'll think about it," she laughed aloud and started to kiss me back.

The next morning, I was dressed and ready to go out. Penny had already gone off to her studio. I wondered if she was going to talk to Gordy. The two of them have worked together for a long time. Gordy had helped her get two shots at a national show. He was a great producer for her.

I looked for Willy, but Penny must have taken him, so I went out to the car. I backed out looking at the motorhome parked on the side of the garage, thinking about our last trip in it.

I arrived at the office and saw Fred out back working in the flower beds. Henry, his dog, was in the dog run on the side of the building. I parked and went by him saying good morning. He smiled and replied. I walked down the hallway when my cell phone buzzed. I took it out as I entered my office. "Hello?" I said, noting there was no caller ID.

"Mr. Richards, this is Sue. Are you busy?"

"No, I just got into my office, what's up?"

"I need a couple of people to sign a form saying that I was instrumental in detaining Conner. It's a formality, but I need it to show that Conner is no longer available to the courts back in Missouri."

"After what you went through, I think you deserve that much. Where are you?"

"I'm at Greg's precinct and I'll be here for a while. I may go back to Missouri later today."

"I'll stop by there and see you," I said. We finished and I went out to the lobby. Lacey was at her desk and looked up to me.

"Are you here to bug me?" she asked.

"Nope, to make you happy, I'm officially retiring."

"I'll believe it when I see it," she replied.

"I just came up to say hello. I'm going to LVPD, so I'll be out."

"Good bye, have a nice day," she laughed.

I shook my head and left. I arrived at the precinct shortly after. I saw Greg standing with Lorelei in the squad room. Plunkitt was standing with some guy in a fancy suit. I came up behind them and stood next to Williams.

"What's up?" I asked Williams.

"They're releasing Plunkitt," he said.

"What?" I said louder than I should have. Everyone looked at me. "Sorry," I said. They all looked back to Plunkitt.

I asked Williams why they were letting him go. He said the lawyer informed them that he was held against his will and beat up.

"The police didn't hold him, it was a few underworld figures," I said.

"Tell them that," Williams said.

I was going to mention it when Plunkitt and his lawyer started to leave.

I yelled across the room, "Hey, Plunkitt. You know when you go out there, there will be people looking for you. They found you once, they can do it again. This time they may not be so easy on you."

The lawyer turned and asked, "Who is this man?"

Lorelei smiled and said, "No one you have to worry about." She looked at Plunkitt, "He's not someone you need to worry about, either. But I think you understand that."

I moved forward. "Plunkitt, you have a safe place here. Why do you want to go out there and face the men who questioned you?"

Plunkitt looked at his lawyer, then at the police. "I think I'll stay."

"Are you surrendering your rights?" Lorelei asked.

He thought on it then nodded his head. Lorelei turned to Greg and said, "Put him back."

The lawyer started to protest but Plunkitt told him to get lost. He frowned and left.

Lonely Hearts Murders

Lorelei came to me and said, "I can't condone the use of mob figures but it helped, so let's not make a big deal out of it. But off the record, thank them for me," she said with a grin and went off to her office.

Sue came over to me and smiled. "Thanks for helping me, this has been a fun ride, not all the time, but most." She held out a folded paper and asked me to sign it. I took it and she showed me where. I folded it back up and handed it to her.

"Is your stuff still in the guest house?" I asked.

"No, I put it all in the rental car. I want to get away from Vegas as soon as possible."

"What about Greg?" I asked.

"He's still a great person but he's changed. Not my kind of guy."

"Well, have a safe trip back. Are you going to say goodbye or just sneak out?"

"Sneak, I hate goodbyes. But for you, I'll make an exception. Take care, Jim. It was nice meeting you." She turned and went out of the squad room.

**

Chapter 24

I almost hated to see her slip out like that. I didn't care for goodbyes either, but there was an emptiness about just going away.

I stood alone in the middle of the squad room watching everyone rushing about. Lorelei was in her new office and I figured Greg was putting Plunkitt in interrogation, since he fired his lawyer.

Lonely Hearts Murders

I went to Lorelei's office and stood at the door until she saw me. "Jim, don't stand out there, come in."

"I was just taking in the fact that Weber isn't here. It's strange after all these years. Good to see you and congratulations on your promotion."

"Thanks, have a seat."

I sat and she sat back asking, "So, how's Penny doing? I heard she had quite an ordeal."

"She's back to normal. The woman amazes me most of the time. She can spring back from the worst fates she can endure."

"She seems to be a strong woman. How's the P.I. business doing?"

"It keeps us running, mostly spousal cheating cases, but they pay, so I'm fine with it. Every so often a murder comes up, like this one. It's not something I want all the time."

"I'd like to see a lot less of that. It's amazing how many murders are committed that the public doesn't know about. We solve most of them, but a lot gets away from us. What are you going to do now since we have Plunkitt in custody and Conner is dead?"

"I've decided to retire. I'm getting older and want to enjoy life, maybe go back to Michigan and see my grandkids before they get too old. I hope I can get away from being a private investigator. It's quite a life."

"It is, that's why I enjoy this job." Her desk phone rang and she answered, listened and then hung up. "Sorry, Jim, but duty calls." We stood and went out of the room.

"Good to have you back," I said.

"Good to see you again, Jim, take care." She went off down the hall and I went back into the squad room again. Everyone was doing their jobs so I turned to the exit and left the building, going back to my car.

Lonely Hearts Murders

I arrived back at the office and decided to sit in the back of the building on the little patio that Fred had set up. The tables and chairs were a nice addition and it was in the shade of the building away from the relentless sun. I never liked the constant gloom of Michigan, it was nice here in Vegas with all the sunshine. Although constant sunshine can get a little unnerving after a while. Unfortunately, when it did rain, there was usually a flood. Six of one, half dozen of another.

I watched Trapper drive in and park. He came over to me and sat. "Enjoying the weather?" he asked.

"It's always the same, most of the time," I replied. "I'm officially retiring," I added.

"What is this, your eighth retirement?" he said with a grin.

"No, the last. After this last adventure and Penny being taken again, I've had it. I can't keep her safe if I'm involving her with killers. So, I'm out of the business."

"Do you have enough money to live on?" he said sitting back.

"Oh, I have plenty. My book sales have been decent over the years and I put away all those earnings. Plus, my income from this place still comes in. I'll have more than enough to live on." I paused, thinking about it. "Penny has a small fortune stashed away, if I run out. We should be happy for a long time."

"I've thought about retiring, too. I'm not much younger than you, but I have enough money squirrelled away to relax."

"You probably have all that cash you saved from your years with the police. I'm sure you probably have some gold stashed away, too."

"I'll never tell. But I do have a treasure map leading to the gold," he said with a laugh.

Lonely Hearts Murders

"Well, don't retire too soon, I'll need you to help run the firm. I'm going to set up a limited partnership with everyone, so you all own a chunk of the business."

"Wow, moving up from employee to management, I'm thrilled," he mugged.

"Yeah, you'd run the business into the ground if I didn't have Earl, Buck, Lynn and Deacon to watch you."

"So, what are you going to do?"

"Travel, I hope. If Penny finally decides to retire. I want to visit every state in the country at least once. There are a few states I'll just drive through," I said as my cell phone buzzed. I saw it was Greg and answered. "Hey, Greg, what's up?"

"Did Sue leave?" he asked me.

"She said she hated to say goodbye, so she's gone."

"Damn, I wanted to tell her some things. Well, it's too late now. Thanks for your help on this mess. It was quite a ride. I got Plunkitt to confess to murdering Keller."

"How'd you manage that?"

He laughed and said, "I told him I would turn him over to your friends. He didn't like that too well. The guy actually wasn't very tough, not a big serial killer like I imagined. Anyway, the case is closed."

"Good, I can tell my daughter now. She was upset over this. Thanks, Greg, and congratulations on your promotion." We finished and hung up.

Trapper laughed. I asked what he was laughing about.

"I was just thinking about the first time we met. You were a thorn in my side, but you did well. We've come a long way, haven't we?"

"We have, now it's time to move on. I'll still be around, just to keep all of you in line."

"I hope so, this place needs you wandering the hallways looking for things to do. I think Lacey would get lonely without you."

"She'll do fine. Well, shall we go in and see what new adventures face us now?"

"I'll do that, you just sit here and enjoy your retirement." He stood and went in.

I sat back and took in the nice weather.

THE END

~~*~~

Bob Moats

Jim Richards Family of Readers

Thanks to the following people who are now part of the Jim Richards Family of Readers. They have read a book or more and enjoyed them. They all volunteered to be included in the list. If you are a fan of the books, send me your full name and you will be included in future books. Send your name to murdernovels@bobmoats.com to be added here and on the website. (updated 05-28-15)

* Achim Feifel * Al Norris * Alex Wheatley * Alexandra Delporte-Wilkinson * Amy Morningstar * Andrea Bryan * Anne Shepherd * Arianda Sugar * Arlene Markowski * Ashley Augustus * Audra Hall * Barbara Hughes * Barbara Sammons * Barbara Schuler * Barbara Zirger * Beth Donohue Plenskofski * Beth Rosin * Betsy Childress * Beth Gibson * Betty Albrecht Vollmar * Bill Sandy * Bill Tornquist * Billie-jo Collie * Bob Lenski * Boni J Rychener * Candace Larson * Carl Bishopric * Carla Lewis * Carole Henderson * Carolyn Conroy * Carolyn Riddle-Linington * Cassy Bailey * Cathie Turner * Chad Hudson * Charlie Meier * Charlotte L Duran * Cheryl L. Everett * Cindy Ackley Nunn *

Lonely Hearts Murders

Cindy Valstad * Connie Bancroft * Corinne Kay
O'Daniel * Chris Krolczyk * Dana Robbins Chuchran
* Dana Wichita * Daniel Kalus * Danielle Monique *
Darren Heald * Dave Travers * David Wilkinson *
David Wiman * DeAnn Jannereth * Deanna Miller *
Deb Breuker Balbo * Deb Chenoweth * Debbie
Carter * Debbie White * Deborah Fartuch * Deborah
Gauze * Deborah Sullivan * Dee King * Denise
Freeman * Devdatta Arun Gholkar * Diana Carver *
Dianna Marie Juneau * Dianne Procopio * Dixie
Beck * Donna Gould * Donna Thompson * Donny
Minter * Doris Kight * Eddie Moore * Eric Walters *
Felicia Annette Bradfield * Fleur Wilkinson *
Francine Menor * Gail Chesney * Georgiann Minster
* George Conner * Greg Colucci * Hayley Rankin *
Harold Garcia * Heidi Arnold * Herb Muir * Irma
Ranee Coy * Jack Plunkitt * Jacqueline Moss * Jan
Kimball * Janet Estep Lawson * Janice Schneider *
Janice Spoor * Jeanette Mulroy * Jennifer Besner *
Jennifer Redmond * Jerry Dornak * Jessica Keown-
Belous * Jim Beck * Jo Boguslaw * Joela Quaine *
Jo Turner * Joanne Marie Turner * Joanna
Wisniewski * John Gross * John Peiffer * John
Wisbiski * Joseph Wauro * Joyce Stacy * Joyce
Trifiletti * Judy Franklin * Judy Travers * Judy
Padgett * Julie Heath * Junnahvee Benson * Karen
Dahl * Karen Grams * Karen Higham * Karen Kaiser
* Karen R. Merritt * Karen Meinburg Richwine *
Karen Kirkman Parker * Karin Hawkins * Karin
Vasvari * Karn Jones * Kathleen Donohue Roesing *
Kathleen Riddle-Wolfe * Kathy Hinds Moore *
Kathy Jones * Kathy Mitchell * Katie Benzler * Kay

Bob Moats

Burns * Kelly Garcia * Ken Boggs * Keota
Rodriguez * Kiera Mccarthy * Kim Estes *
Kimberley May * Kitty Stolle * Kristie Sciler *
Kirsty Stanton * LaLonnie Scallen * Larry Morris *
Leann Parr * Lenora Scales * Leslie Marie Jackson *
Linda Forester * Linda Bartley Florence * Linda
Ingle Cox * Linda Kennerö * Linda Magill * Lisa
Bower * Lisa Keller * Liz Gibson * Lorraine Wiman
* Loretta Alexander * Lynda Bowles * Lynette
Lawrance * LuAnn Louttit * Manny Rothman *
Marcia-Lee Finocchio * Marcia Gibson DeWitt *
Marie Calder * Marlene Bryan * MaryLouise Kramp
* Mary Lynn Gross * Megan Atkins * Meghan
Hyden * Melissa Wescoat * Melody Cannavan *
Meredith Simko Hanak * Michael Carruthers *
Michael Dinkens * Michael Vannoy * Michelle
Burns-Mitchell * Michelle Pilcher * Micki Potter *
Mike Moats * Mikki Gregory * Mimi Baur * Merri
Taylor * Myrna Hecht * Nadine Sutton * Nancy
Ellen Sayre * Nancy Graveman Davis * Natalie
Quine * Neena Martin * O'Della Wilson * Pamela
Cooke Malone-O'brien * Pat Pollington * Pat Rohn *
Patricia Jarmon * Patricia C Trezza * Patrick Barry *
Paul Lawrance * Peggy Davis * Phyllis Bassett * Ray
Zink * Raylene Matheny * Rebecca Collins Besner *
Renee Brumley * Reta Hanna * Reta Moats * Robert
Lenski * Roberta Meister * Roberta Navarro-Harder
* Sally Berneathy * Sally Hubler * Sandy Sillman *
Sandy Schuman * Sara Swope * Sarah Santos *
Satka Nikc * Sharon E. Edwards * Sharon Mangini *
Sharon McMillon * Sheena Rawl * Sherry Amstutz *
Sherry Tull * Shirley Alvarez * Shirley Davies *

Lonely Hearts Murders

Shirley Williams * Stacie Rowe * Stephanie Conner * Steve Cullen * Sue Payne * Susan Haughton * Susan Hesse Adams * Susan Salomon * Suzan K Chase * Taisha Cullum * Tamara Moore * Tammy Castleberry * Tammy Lynn Wood * Ted Murphy * Terri Atkins * Terri Creech * Terry Raab * Theresa Miracle Harmon * Tonia Rachael Riggs-Williams * Tonya Mann * Travis Fleury-Lopez * Twyla Gawlas * Val Brooks * Walt Munsel * Yvonne Isakson *

Thank you to all these wonderful people.

Thank you for purchasing this book. I hope you enjoy it as much as I enjoyed writing it for my faithful readers. Please feel free to email me to tell me what you thought about my stories. I love hearing from the readers. I can be reached at murdernovels@bobmoats.com thanks again!

*